Discovery

Discovery

The Wanderton Chronicles

Ashley Yule

Library of Congress Control Number: 2019903301
ISBN: Hardcover   978-1-7960-2243-8
               Softcover   978-1-7960-2242-1
               eBook   978-1-7960-2241-4

Print information available on the last page.

Rev. date: 03/19/2019

To order additional copies of this book, contact:
Xlibris
1-888-795-4274
www.Xlibris.com
Orders@Xlibris.com
793291

CONTENTS

Chapter 1   The Visitors 1

Chapter 2   The Academy 7

Chapter 3   Gertrude and Her Crew 12

Chapter 4   The Arrival of the First Years 17

Chapter 5   Exploring the Academy 21

Chapter 6   Familiars and Abilities 25

Chapter 7   Familiars and Abilities 30

Chapter 8   After the Ceremony 35

Chapter 9   Classes 40

Chapter 10   Regeneration with the Headmaster and Warrior
             Tryouts 46

Chapter 11   Letters 53

Chapter 12   Confessions of Feelings 59

Chapter 13   Learning More Information 65

Chapter 14   A Saturday Afternoon and a Full Moon 69

Chapter 15   An Attack 73

Chapter 16   Learning More About Last Night 77

Chapter 17   A Plan...82

Chapter 18   Sniffing Out the Culprit 87

Chapter 19   A Favor and Dresses 92

Chapter 20   The Dance 97

Chapter 21   Another Attack 102

Chapter 22   Finding Out Who Is Behind the Attacks 107

Chapter 23   Happy Love Day 111

Chapter 24   Time Gone By and a Surprise 116

Chapter 25   Telling the Academy 120

Chapter 26   Taking a Ride 125

Chapter 1

The Visitors

It was a warm sunny day, and there was a nice, cool breeze. Everlee was lying in the garden, watching the clouds go by, trying to find pictures in the sky. It was just then that there was a loud trumpet blaring, signaling an important visitor. Everlee, being curious, got up and ran back inside the castle.

Everlee was Wanderton's princess, beloved by all in her kingdom. She was fourteen years old, five feet four, with beautiful big brown eyes and brown hair with honey-brown highlights flowing to the middle of her back, pale skin, and freckles on her face and shoulders. She was very gorgeous and kind.

Meanwhile, back to Everlee as she ran through the back door by the garden and sped up and around the corridors till she got to the main hall. She stopped. There was a brigade of people there.

"Everlee, darling, I know you're somewhere nearby. Please come over here, darling," said her mother.

A bit embarrassed, Everlee walked out from behind the back pillar and walked over to her mother and father's side. Her mother was so beautiful, with long blond hair and gorgeous blue eyes, and her father had dark-brown hair to his shoulders and brown eyes.

"Good day, my darling," said her father.

"Your Majesty," said Lieutenant Green, "I have reason to believe we may be in for a war soon with the wolves. Their leader, the alpha Sir Edgar, refuses to get a sizable group under control. They are changing at will and with no regard for safety and killing in numbers. I'm afraid if we don't stop it, we'll have a bloodbath. The vampires are growing uneasy too, sire. The wolves are getting closer to their territory, and the vampires could attack back in retaliation. There's also the safety of the academy to think about there in the middle of the wolves' path, and the elves are growing nervous as well. The dwarfs are still keeping to themselves for now."

Just then, one of the soldiers spoke out, "But why do we have to go to war? It's not our problem."

King Jasper held up his hand. "It is our business. If we don't stop this, we ourselves could be in danger too, especially if the clans were to break into war. It can easily spill over. Plus, as king, it is my duty to protect this land and everyone in it."

Everlee's mother, Queen Grace, squeezed the king's hand and gave him a knowing nod. After the king finished speaking, Lieutenant Green had the soldier taken down to the dungeon area. "I'll be there shortly for reprimanding, and if my king would join me?" he asked, looking at him.

King Jasper nodded. "I will," he said.

Later that night, Everlee sat on her balcony, trying to process all that she'd heard being discussed earlier. Suddenly, there was a knock on the door.

"Come in," she called, and then in walked her handmaiden and childhood friend, Sandy. She had beautiful blue eyes and light-brown hair to her shoulders. Sandy and her mom lived in the castle. She and Everlee grew up together, and even though she was a staff, she and Everlee were the best of friends.

Sandy walked over to her. "Evie, are you okay? I caught wind that a brigade showed up, and there was talk of possibly going to war and that you may leave."

Everlee sighed. "You heard right. There very well might be a war soon if we can't stop the wolves that have gone rogue. Their leader, Sir Edgar, is refusing to stop it, and we can't understand why. He has always been so sensible and a good leader. We're gonna try again to reason with him, although there is a rumor in the brigade that there may be something else going on behind the leader 'cause the behavior isn't like him. My dad's worried, I can tell, even though he tries to hide it."

Sandy took a deep breath. "And the rumor I heard about you leaving?"

Everlee turned her head for a moment. She didn't want Sandy to see her tear-filled eyes. She took a deep breath and turned to Sandy. "I'm afraid it's true. I leave in two days for the academy. If we do come to war, I need to be prepared, and so, yes, Sandy, I do have to go, but I'm gonna learn and do my family and kingdom proud."

Suddenly, Sandy hugged her. "I know you will. I'm gonna miss you. Write to me, please, so that until you come back, we will still have each other to talk to."

"Of course, I will," said Everlee.

The next morning, Everlee was sitting at the table with her parents.

"Everlee, darling," her mother said, "I know you're scared, but just know that you are strong and wise. We know you'll do amazing. If the danger gets out of hand near the school, we'll send help."

Everlee nodded. She didn't know what else to say, so nodding seemed appropriate.

Later that night, as she lay in bed, she couldn't help but think about what tomorrow would bring. She would be going to the academy. A part of her was nervous yet excited, but the other part felt concerned. She should be staying here with her family and kingdom with the danger looming. She tried to plead this earlier, but her parents kept insisting that she needed to go train and learn. She supposed they were right, but she was going to miss them.

As she lay there trying to sleep, she imagined what the academy would be like. Would she fit in? And on that note, she drifted off to sleep.

Suddenly, there was a knock on the door. "Ms. Everlee? It's time to wake up, madam, it's time to get dressed and then go down for breakfast, before you leave in an hour. I'll bring your luggage down for you."

Everlee sat up and stretched. *Well, time for the adventure to begin,* she thought, and up she got. A few minutes later, she was down eating breakfast. She didn't have much of an appetite, so she just had a bowl of oatmeal with some honey and a glass of milk. Suddenly, her parents were in the dining hall's doorway.

"Everlee, darling," her mother began, "honey, I know things seem all jumbled right now and don't really make a lot of sense, but can we talk, please, for a few minutes before you leave?"

"I know you're upset, but you need to hear this, hon," her father, King Jasper, said.

"Yes, my darling, we must talk, especially before you leave. Truth be told, we should have told you a long time ago."

Everlee just stared at her parents in disbelief. What in the world? What was so important? "Okay, sure."

"Wonderful," said her mother. "Finish your breakfast, then meet us in the study, please." They turned and walked away, leaving Everlee there reeling in her own thoughts.

What should I have been told a long time ago? Is it something to do with me leaving? Why are they now telling me? So many thoughts. She could feel her head start to throb. "Calm down, Evie," she said, giving herself a bit of a pep talk. "You're strong and just need to breathe. Surely whatever the big secret is, they had their reasons."

A few moments later, Everlee was knocking on her father's study. "Enter," he called, and she walked in and closed the door behind her. She saw that it wasn't just her parents in the study. There were two other people there: an older man, probably thirty years older than her parents, and a girl who couldn't be more than a year older than Everlee was. The girl had wavy red hair to the middle of her back, green eyes, and pale skin. The older man had black hair streaked with silver to his shoulders and tied in a ponytail.

"Everlee, please take a seat," her father said, so she made her way to the chair by the fireplace while the rest sat on the couch facing her.

"Hello, Everlee, my name is Headmaster Lional, and this is one of our top students," the old man said, motioning to the girl.

"Hi," she said, "my name is Rachel. I'm gonna be your mentor at the school, and hopefully, we can be friends too." She finished with a smile. Everlee liked her already. She seemed so sweet.

"Right," her father said and cleared his throat. "Evie, this may seem strange sending you off in the middle of all the danger rearing its head, but it's because you're so special that I'm afraid we must." He paused, seemingly unsure of how to proceed.

Her mother squeezed his hand. "Sweetheart," she said, looking at Everlee, "you're special, and I don't just mean in the way of we love you, which, yes, we do. I mean that you have gifts. That's what the academy is for—it's for people who are special and for warriors."

"Special gifts? What are you talking about?" Everlee asked.

"Evie," her mother began, "me and a few other members on my side have gifts, along with your father and his family, some members do as well. We figured that you would too since both your father and I have gifts, but we have no idea what. When you were little, I caught you once. You were two years old, you touched a rosebush outside and made it bloom. It was so gorgeous."

"Then," her father began, "when you were three, I saw you walk on the water in the fountain. It was amazing, yet it scared me. Then we heard of a prophecy. A young girl born in the winter with a birthmark in the shape of the sun on her foot, which you have by the way, would go on to become one of the most remarkable of her time and have so much magical potential. There were some that would have sought you out, tried to kill you, to take out any threat to them or taken you and turned you bad. We didn't know for sure that it was you, but we had a feeling. So we brushed it off to you that you must have fallen asleep and dreamed that you did those things. We then took you to a friend who blocked your memories of that—Headmaster Lional actually. We're so sorry. We just wanted to keep you safe. Please try to understand that. But with this danger looming, I fear that we may need your gifts. Our kingdom and clans, we'll all need you, even if things settle down. We think it's time you left to go train. We don't know what all your gifts are—most only have one gift—but you'll find out soon."

"You're extraordinary, my darling, and some will be jealous and try to make it hard for you, I'm sure, but just stay strong."

Everlee sat there. *Wow,* she thought, *I definitely didn't see this coming.* "Listen," she began, "I'm not mad. I wish you hadn't lied, but I get why you did, but no more lies." They nodded and agreed.

Headmaster Lional spoke up, "If I may, I believe it's time to give back your memories." He yanked out a vial filled with a brown substance. "Here, drink this. Best to chug it fast. I'm afraid it tastes pretty gross, but it'll do the job."

Everlee uncorked the vial and chugged it down. He wasn't lying; it really was nasty. Suddenly, she felt lightheaded and felt like the room was spinning, and the next thing she knew, everything went black. Suddenly, it was like she was watching a show in her head as she watched herself in her memories. Just then, it felt like she was being yanked back, and she was blinking up at her parents, Headmaster Lional, and Rachel.

"Sorry about that," said Lional. "Sometimes the side effects include fainting." He helped her up. "Well, we better get going. Is Sandy ready too?" Lional asked her father.

"Huh? Sandy?" she asked. "Why would Sandy be going?" *Not that I'd mind,* she thought. *She'd love it, to be honest.*

"You'll have time to ask her yourself," Headmaster Lional said. "We really must be going now."

Chapter 2

The Academy

Sandy walked in, ran to Evie, and hugged her. "Oh my goodness, I can't believe that I get to go too."

"Yeah, about that, how come you get to go?" Evie asked. "Not that I'm upset, I am actually really happy."

Sandy told her that last night when she was doing the dusting and taking a break for a moment, because she was upset that Evie was leaving, she closed her eyes as she cried, and suddenly, she felt wet. When she opened them, there was a rain cloud over her head. The headmaster, who had gotten there last night, saw it and how it vanished when he surprised her. "He told me that it looked like I would be going today as well, that I have a gift. Oh my goodness! I didn't expect this, Evie," she said. "He said that sometimes gifts can show up later and also if we're in an emotional state. But I get to go with you!" Sandy beamed.

Everlee was so excited and surprised. Man, today was really turning into an adventure, and they hadn't even left for the academy yet.

Suddenly, Headmaster Lional came over. "Well, let's go, ladies. Sandy, your mom said goodbye already?"

"Yes," Sandy said.

"Very well—oh, Sandy, this is Rachel," he said. "She'll be Everlee's mentor, and I'm sure you all will become friends." Sandy and Rachel smiled at each other.

"How are we getting there?" Everlee asked. "By carriage?"

"No, I have something far more magical," he said with a wink and a twinkle in his eyes. Everlee and Sandy looked at each other, then at Headmaster Lional as he pulled out something so amazing. It was like a small spinning, sparkly blue-and-green circle. He took it, put it in the closet, and said a few whispered words, so low Everlee didn't catch it—but knew he had because she saw him whisper—then he closed the closet door, turned his head to them, winked, and then looked back and opened the closet. Suddenly, her father's closet was gone, and inside was some sort of swirling vortex. It was so gorgeous.

"What's that?" Sandy asked before Evie could.

"It's a portal. It'll take us to my office at the academy. Now, Everlee, please say your goodbyes, dear. The luggage has been sent on already while you were eating breakfast. Yours too, Sandy."

Everlee turned and hugged her parents. "What is your gift?" she asked.

"I have the gift of earth," said her father.

"And I am gifted with water," said her mother. Evie looked confused. "Don't worry," her mom said. "You'll understand soon."

"Goodbye, sweetie. We love you, and we'll miss you," they said.

"Come, come," Lional called, "we don't have long before it closes."

Rachel, Lional, Evie, and Sandy stood next to the closet. "I'll go first and show you how it's done," said Rachel, and with that, she walked into the closet and disappeared.

"Sandy, you next," said Lional, and just like Rachel, Sandy disappeared too. "Evie, now you." With one last look at her parents, Everlee walked in. It felt like she was being sucked in a tight tube, but it didn't hurt. Next thing Everlee knew, she was falling out onto the floor of Headmaster Lional's office. She looked up to see Rachel's hand.

"Here," she said, pulling Evie to her feet. "You okay? The first few times are kinda weird, but after a bit, you'll just be able to walk out instead of fall." She smiled.

"Thanks," Everlee said. She looked over and saw Sandy sitting in a chair by the desk, holding her head. "You okay?" Evie asked her.

"Yeah," said Sandy, "just lightheaded." She grinned.

Evie looked around. The walls were full of books and other trinkets that looked interesting. The desk was a beautiful cherry with intricate carvings on the edges. There was also a sitting area by the fireplace across the room. Suddenly, out walked Headmaster Lional from the closet. He closed the door, whispered something, then opened the door again, and put the orb thing back in his pocket. "I'll put this away later." He smiled. "Your luggage is by the fireplace."

Huh? Evie thought. She turned and looked. How had she overlooked that before? Weird.

"So now what?" asked Sandy.

This time, Headmaster Lional nodded at Rachel. Rachel spoke up, "Now you follow me." She smiled. "I'll take you to your room. There are two to a room, so you and Sandy will be roommates. My room is just down the hall from yours. Follow me, please, it's almost lunchtime." So they grabbed their luggage—even Rachel helped them carry the luggage—and followed Rachel out of the office.

"Goodbye, my dears, I'll see you later," called Lional.

"Goodbye!" they chorused.

As they walked down the hallway and out into another hall, Rachel spoke to Sandy, "Your mentor's my roommate, Lacey. You'll meet her later, but she's very nice. A bit shy, but she's great."

Sandy nodded. She and Evie were both in awe. The place was huge. The walls were some type of black stone, not smooth and shiny, but more like rough stone. The floors were this pretty maple wood, and there were lots of windows.

"Where are the students?" Evie asked.

"Oh, they're in their classes. It's almost lunchtime though, so pretty soon, the halls will get crowded." She smiled.

As they were rounding a corner, Evie banged into something solid and warm. She fell on her butt and looked up. There, standing above her, was the most handsome boy she had ever seen. He had tan skin, piercing green eyes, and jet-black hair.

"I'm so sorry," he started. He helped her back up. "My name's Dametri."

"What are you up to?" said Rachel, grinning in amusement.

"I was just heading to see the headmaster. I had a note to meet him at his office. Well, before I go, can I get your names? I've never seen you two before, new students?"

They nodded. "Yes, I'm Everlee, and this is Sandy." Everlee gestured to her friend; Sandy grinned.

"Well, it was lovely to meet you. I'm afraid I must be going, but I hope to see you later." Evie nodded, and with that, Dametri took off and vanished around the corner.

"Oh my gosh!" Rachel squealed. "He was totally checking you out." Sandy nodded at Evie, smiling too.

"What? No, he wasn't . . . was he?"

"Uh, duh," Rachel said, then smiled. "Look out though, a lot of girls fancy him, so be prepared for some jealous bimbos later."

Evie nodded. Man was he cute. She hoped they were right. If he really did like her, oh that would be amazing. But she reminded herself that she should get to know him first.

"Well, this way, girls," said Rachel. They walked down a flight of stairs and down a hall with numbered doors and oil lamps hanging on brass bars from the walls. They stopped at the end of the hall at number 13. "Here's your room, girls." Rachel opened the door, and inside were two twin-sized beds, a beautiful chandelier with crystals and candles for the light, two nightstands, and a pretty maple-wood desk in between the beds. The room was painted a pretty purple color. The beds had a cream-colored and light-purple bedding, and there was a window by the little sitting area, with two big tan-colored chairs and a round table in between. The closet was a walk-in with a four-drawer dresser in the back of it and a mirror on the closet door. "You guys will have to share the closet," Rachel piped up.

"That's fine," Sandy and Evie chorused. Both of them loved the room.

"Well, if you want to unpack really quick and get settled in, I'll be back in a little bit to take you down to lunch. Oh, and the bathroom for us girls is actually across the hall. If you step outside, it's the door across from yours." Rachel smiled and, with that, closed the door.

"Oh my gosh," said Sandy.

"I know," said Evie. "I can't believe we're gonna be roommates."

"I know," said Sandy. "This is so amazing. I hope people will like me."

"They will, I know it," said Evie. "Well, we should hurry and unpack."

"Yeah," agreed Sandy. "Hey, can I have the top two dresser drawers?"

"Yeah, sure," said Evie, and with that, they got to work unpacking, and about forty minutes later, there was a knock on the door.

"Hey, guys, can I come in?" called Rachel.

"Yes, come on in," called Evie, and in walked Rachel.

"You guys all done? It's time for lunch, if you guys are hungry."

"Sounds great," said Sandy.

"Yeah," said Evie.

"Okay, cool, let's go. Oh, here are your room keys, one for you both," she said as she handed them over.

"Thanks," they chorused.

"Okay, let's go." With that, they followed Rachel out of their room. Evie locked the door, and down the hall they went.

Chapter 3

Gertrude and Her Crew

As the girls walked down the hall and up the stairs, a thought ran through Everlee's head. "Rachel?" she called.

"Yes?" Rachel replied.

"I was wondering," Everlee started, "are we the only new students? Are more coming? How long do people go here? Can you tell me more about the academy, and when do we find out what our gifts are and how?"

Rachel smiled. "Well, no, you're not the only new students. The others will be arriving after lunch, and by dinner, everyone should be here. There will be a welcome dinner for the school, first years come a week after the other students. There are lots to explain, but how about we get to lunch first, then we can talk and eat."

Evie nodded. Sandy, meanwhile, was looking around, and suddenly, she piped up, "So how many boys are there here?"

Rachel laughed. "A good number," she said. Sandy smiled. "Oh, Sandy, Lacey is meeting us at lunch, so you'll get to finally meet her," Rachel added.

Sandy smiled. "Great! I hope she likes me."

"Oh, I'm sure she will," replied Rachel. "She's shy at first and kinda quiet, but she's very nice and kind."

Rachel led them up the stairs, down another hall, down another flight of stairs, and into a hall without any windows, just oil lamps hanging from brass bars from the walls. "The dining hall is just down at the end of the hall behind those doors." She pointed at two big cherry doors with brass rings for the knobs. Rachel opened the door. Inside it were thirty large round tables, big enough to fit eight people per table, and a long table up front where the headmaster and whom Everlee assumed must be where the teachers were sitting. The ceiling had five huge circular brass chandeliers with candles for the lights, and there was a line of students off to the left side.

"What's that line?" Evie asked.

Rachel led them over to the line. "This is where we line up and grab our food. There are trash bins on the right side of the hall in the back corner."

"Well, hello again," came a familiar voice from behind Everlee. She turned around; it was Dametri. She smiled.

"Hi," she replied.

"So how are you liking it so far?" he asked.

"It's nice. I mean, I haven't been here very long, but I think I'm gonna like it here. I am missing my parents," Evie admitted.

Dametri put his hand on her shoulder. "Hey, that's okay. I missed my dad when I first came here. I still do sometimes. If you ever want to talk, I'm here." He grinned.

Everlee nodded. "Thanks," she said. "If I may ask, what about your mom?"

His smile disappeared, and suddenly, he looked sad. "She died when I was young."

"Oh, I'm so sorry," Evie said, feeling terrible for bringing up something so painful.

"It's okay," he said. "I still have Dad and my older brother, Wyatt, and older sister, Anne. They're home with Dad. They don't have gifts, and sometimes I think Wyatt is jealous even though he denies it. He's next in line for the throne, provided he can beat me and my sister this summer in the fight for beta, but until then, he's acting beta." Evie gave him a weird look. "Oh, I'm sorry," he said. "I should explain—my dad's Sir Edgar, leader of the wolves."

Evie gasped. "You're a wolf?"

"Yes," he replied.

"Oh," she gasped. "No, I'm sorry, I didn't mean to be rude. I'm just surprised. I've never met a wolf before."

"It's okay," he said.

"You know," Evie started, "a lot of people are worried about a group of rogue wolves."

Dametri had a dark look come over him. "Yeah, I heard about that. It isn't like my father to allow that. He's a great man."

"I heard that he was," Evie replied. "What do you think is going on?"

"I have no idea," he replied, "but hopefully, it's resolved soon. I don't want people to hate our clan—we're not all like that."

Evie touched his shoulder this time. "I believe you." He smiled at her.

Suddenly, a female voice from behind Dametri yelled out, "Hey, Dametri, come sit with us!" Evie looked, and sitting at a table near the back was a group of four girls and three guys.

"Hey, Gertie," Dametri called out. Gertie smiled at him and waved. She was olive-skinned and had long black hair to her butt and had hazel eyes. Dametri responded, "I'm gonna sit with Evie today, okay?"

"Oh," Gertie responded, "okay." As soon as Dametri looked away, Gertie gave Everlee a death glare before turning to the girl next to her, presumably to talk about her, seeing as how they kept looking and pointing at her.

Evie turned back to Dametri. "Who's that?"

"Oh, that's Gertrude," he said, "but I call her Gertie and so do her friends."

"You guys aren't a couple, are you?" Evie asked.

"Me and Gertie? No." He laughed. "Just friends."

"I think she likes you," Evie said.

"What makes you say that?" he asked.

"'Cause of the death glare I got after you turned her down."

"Huh, really? I can talk to her about it," he offered.

"No, please, I don't want to make it worse."

"Okay," he said, "but if it keeps up, please let me know."

Evie nodded. A few minutes later, they had reached the front, and she saw that there were pans of food with little balls of fire under them. There were beef stew, pork chops, veggies, fried chicken, and mashed potatoes.

"Are the cooks gifted?" she asked.

"Yep," he grinned.

She grabbed a tray and took a bowl of stew and a glass of milk. "So do vampires go here too?" Evie asked.

"Of course," he said, "but it's cool. Most are friendly. They take night classes, so our dinner is their breakfast, and they drink animal blood. They'll be out later tonight."

She smiled at him. Sandy and Rachel turned around. "Dametri, are you gonna sit with us?"

"If you'll have me." He grinned.

"Of course," Rachel said. With that, they walked off in search of a table. "Oh, there's Lacey," Rachel said, pointing across the hall to the right. When they got to the table and sat down, Rachel introduced them. "Guys, this is my roommate, Lacey. Sandy, this is your mentor."

Sandy smiled and waved. "Hi," she said.

"Hi," Lacey answered, smiling. "I'm sorry I wasn't able to meet you before now."

"That's okay," said Sandy.

"Hi," Lacey said to Evie.

"Hi, I'm Everlee, it's nice to meet you," she replied, smiling.

"Hey, Lacey," Dametri said.

"Hey, Dametri, how are you?"

"I'm all right," he said, "and you?"

"Can't complain," she said.

Evie looked at Lacey; she seemed nice. Lacey was an elf. She had pointy ears, pale blond, almost white hair to the middle of her back, pale skin, and gorgeous dark-blue eyes. They sat and enjoyed lunch, and Rachel explained how the headmaster handpicks the mentors each year for the first-year students. Mentors at least had to be a second year;

they went to school there for four years. Rachel, Lacey, and Dametri were all second years.

"What about finding out what our gifts are?" Evie asked.

Lacey smiled. "That's easier to find out in person. Don't worry, it's coming up soon. Tonight, after the welcome dinner, you guys and the rest of the first years will find out. The whole school will be there too. It's held outside. It's okay, though try not to be nervous."

"What about the warriors?" Sandy asked.

Dametri spoke up, "That is something for the brave and wise. There are tests, and if you pass, you can join. I'm actually a warrior myself. You're able to be a warrior and gifted—you don't have to be separate. They're our protectors." Evie and Sandy grinned at each other. This was so cool.

The bell sounded; time to clear out. "Everyone else has got class, but mentors are to take first years to the west wing to meet the other new students. But I think it's just you guys so far. Everyone else will be arriving in a few minutes. Let's go." They threw their food away, and Dametri came too.

"You're a mentor?" Evie asked.

"Yep, I just have to meet him. I have some guy named Kyle."

Suddenly, Gertrude and her crew came up to Evie. "Can I talk to you?" she asked.

"Sure," Evie said. She didn't like the vibe she was getting.

Gertrude pulled her to the side. "Listen, this is my turf, and you need to stay away from Dametri. I want to ask him out."

Evie had enough. "With all due respect, shouldn't that be his call?"

Gertrude glared. "Listen, just because—"

She was cut off. Sandy and her group had come up.

"Everything okay?" Dametri asked.

"Of course," Gertrude said, smiling. "Well, I gotta go. Bye, Dametri." She walked over to her crew and, with a glare toward Evie, walked off.

Rachel leaned over and whispered in Evie's ear, "I told you there would be jealous bimbos." Evie just shook her head.

"Well, let's go," said Lacey, and off down the hall they went.

Chapter 4

The Arrival of the First Years

Everlee and Sandy and the rest of her group walked up the hall and stairs and made a detour to the right of the hallway. There, just before they went down, was a brass door with a crystal doorknob.

"Where does the door lead to?" asked Sandy.

Lacey spoke up, "It's where the first years come in. There's another one down in the dungeons, for vampire students." She smiled. "Let's go meet them. I'll go first," she said, and with that, she opened the door. Inside was a spiral staircase. They all followed her inside. Dametri was last and closed the door.

They made their way up the staircase. There were windows spaced a few feet apart along the way for light. Everlee looked out. *We must be in a tower,* she thought. Outside, she saw a beautiful waterfall, and she wanted to stop and see more out the window, but Rachel touched her shoulder. "Come on, Evie, I know it's pretty outside. You'll go out there soon, but for now, let's keep going."

"Okay," Evie said, nodding.

They reached the top and walked into a circular room with maple-wood floor and eight fireplaces around it. Inside were Headmaster Lional and five other students.

"Hello." He smiled at them. "These are the rest of the mentors. We only have ten new students this year," he said.

"Why so little?" asked Dametri.

"Oh, each year's different. Some have more, some have less. We already have two here." He nodded to Sandy and Evie. "The other six will be here soon." He saw the look on Evie's face. "Ah," he said, "forgive me, there are two vampire students coming just before dinner. I'll get them later, and their mentors will join me in waiting for them.

Fellow vampires. Oh, that made more sense, she thought.

"How are they getting here?" Sandy asked. Rachel and the other mentors all laughed.

Lacey piped up, "You'll see. It's how most of us came here, with the exception of you two and a few others." She grinned.

Headmaster Lional pulled out a pocket watch and flipped it open. "Ah yes, it is time." He pulled out the spinning orb once more. "Wait in the center with the new students," he instructed. "I'll return once they're all here." He walked over to a fireplace to the right, tossed the orb in, recited his spell, and just like before, opened up the beautiful vortex, all shiny. He stepped in and vanished, along with the vortex.

Suddenly, all the eight fireplaces lit up with this beautiful gold flame. Dametri whispered in Everlee's ear, "It's a transport spell. He's going to each student's home to let them know how to get here."

After a few minutes, out walked six students with their luggage.

"How come they didn't fall out like we did?" Sandy asked.

"The transport spell is gentler than the vortex," Rachel explained. The mentors all ushered the new students to the center of the room. Suddenly, the same fireplace the headmaster left in changed back to a vortex and out he walked. As soon as he shut the vortex off and put it in his pocket, the fireplaces all went out, as if nothing had been just burning.

"So strange," Everlee whispered. Rachel chuckled.

"All right now," Headmaster Lional started, "before you make your way down to your dorms to get settled before dinner, let's get you paired up with your mentors." He yanked out a scroll and unrolled it. "Now, there are five boys and five girls in your group, that's counting the two students joining us later, two of which have already been paired. You will be paired with a mentor of the same sex. Kyle," he called to a tall boy with blond hair, striking dark-green eyes, and pointy ears—an elf. Kyle walked forward. "Ah, Kyle, you will be with Dametri." Dametri stepped forward and shook his hand.

A few minutes later, the others had been paired. "Very well," Lional began, "As I've told you all, this academy is a place for the gifted and the warriors. I'll see you all later at dinner." He smiled. "After dinner, you will learn what your gifts are. Now mentors," he said, "please take the first years to their dorms after introductions are made." With that, he walked off.

"Strange," said Hannah, one of the first years.

"You'll get used to it," said another mentor. "It's great here."

The three other guys were Jack, Robert, and Aiden, and the other girl was Grace. Everyone stood around, talking for a few minutes, getting acquainted, before Dametri spoke up. "Okay, everyone, we should all get going. Let's show them to their dorm rooms." With that, everyone proceeded down the stairs, out of the brass door, and went in different directions with their mentors. Well, all except for Everlee, Sandy, Lacey, Rachel, Dametri, and now Kyle, who seemed friendly.

"What do we do now?" Sandy asked Lacey.

"Well, the mentors have the day to be with the first years. Like I said before, I'm sorry I wasn't with you earlier, but you were in good hands with Rachel. Anyway, now we can explore the grounds and castle if you want.

Before Sandy could reply, Dametri piped up, "Well, I'm gonna take Kyle to his room, but maybe we'll catch up later." He grinned, and with that, the boys headed off.

"So how about exploring?" Lacey asked again.

"Yes," Evie and Sandy said in unison. Rachel and Lacey grinned.

"Okay, then let's go," said Lacey, and off they went down the hallway to the right again, up the stairs, then down the hall. At the end of the hall were two big green doors with brass knobs.

"What's that?" asked Everlee.

"It's the library," said Rachel. They opened the doors and walked inside. It was so beautiful. There were so many books, walls full of them, and there were three floors in there. There was a staircase to each floor, and the walls on each floor had ladders connected to a bar to glide across and get them. The ceiling was a beautiful glass dome. There were desks with oil lamps on them, and the floor was this pretty green stone, so shiny. There was a fireplace in the back with wingback chairs, a set of two of them, and a couch all in black. The librarian's desk was by the eastern window.

"Wow!" Sandy and Everlee echoed.

"Yeah," said Rachel. "This place has so much. We love it here."

"Yes, we come here often," said Lacey. "Well, let's get back to exploring. We'll be back here again soon, I'm sure." She grinned, and they left the library.

Lacey showed them where the classrooms were. They were on their way outside when Sandy asked about the dungeons.

"We don't go down there in the day—that would be rude. They're sleeping. It's not bad though. It's just as pretty down there. It's just darker, that's all."

"Come on, you guys," called Lacey. She was waiting by the back.

"Don't we go out the front?" asked Evie.

"No," said Lacey, "the best views are in the back." She smiled. "Let's go." With that, they opened a set of maple doors with brass knobs and walked outside.

Chapter 5

Exploring the Academy

Everlee and Sandy, along with Rachel and Lacey, were standing in the back of the academy. It was so pretty. There was the usual grass on the ground, and there were pine trees and a vegetable garden—a huge one on the right side, with a little white fence around it—and at least thirty different fruit trees and a few bushes of blueberries, strawberries, and a few other types too. The left-hand side had a gazebo with flowers all around it. Then straight ahead was a walking path; they walked straight ahead. On the other end of the path was an outdoor fighting and training area with climbing walls, floor mats, and so many other things.

"Wow!" said Sandy.

"Yes," said Lacey, "this is where the warriors train—one place anyway. They have a spot inside too."

"Nice," said Everlee. She wasn't gonna say it out loud yet, but she wanted to learn more about the warriors; it piqued her interest.

"Over here," Rachel called, leading them to the right of the mats. There was another path; they walked it, and at the end was the beautiful waterfall Evie saw from the window earlier. It was even prettier up close. Rachel smiled. "Come on, this way."

They walked over to the edge of the waterfall, and Rachel piped up, "This is where the ceremony will be held tonight."

"I'm so nervous," said Sandy.

"Don't be," Dametri said from behind them, making them jump. "Oh, I'm sorry." Dametri and Kyle were standing there. "Kyle finished unpacking, and so I thought I'd show him around. He wanted to see the outdoors first. Hi, Everlee." He smiled. Evie could feel a blush coming on. "So like I said, don't be nervous," Dametri carried on.

"Easier said than done."

"I know, but it's gonna be okay." He smiled.

"Thanks," said Sandy with a nervous grin. "So, Kyle, what is it like back in your clan?"

Kyle grinned. "It's very beautiful. We love to enjoy nature. Would you like to take a walk with me?"

Sandy smiled. "That would be nice."

"Okay." And off they walked.

"Oh, Evie," Sandy yelled back to her, "come get me when you're ready to go in." Evie nodded.

Dametri laughed. "Well, mind if I tag along?"

The girls smiled. "Yes, you may," Rachel said. So they walked along, chatting and laughing for a bit. Evie saw the stables and a field of wildflowers, and there were other trails, but they didn't go down then. "You will someday," Rachel said.

After a little bit, they tracked down Kyle and Sandy and went back inside. "See you later," Kyle and Dametri said as they parted. Rachel and Lacey took Evie and Sandy to their room. "We'll come get you just before dinner. We have two more people coming in."

"See you," Everlee said as they waved and walked off.

"So," Everlee said to Sandy, "how was the walk with Kyle?"

Sandy blushed. "It was nice," she said. "He's very kind."

Evie and Sandy talked and laughed. It seemed time flew because next thing they knew, they heard Rachel and Lacey knocking, and off they went to the dungeons to welcome there other fellow peers. They were back in the hall that went to the dining hall. Just before they went in, there was a door to the left. Evie and her group went inside and down a flight of stairs.

"I'll lead the way," said Rachel. As they followed her, Evie noted that the dungeons weren't scary; they looked just like upstairs, only there were no windows, just oil lamps and some torches for light. They arrived at a brass door with a crystal knob, and inside was the headmaster and the other peers and mentors. They stood in the center.

"I'll be back," said the headmaster, and just like earlier, he disappeared into the vortex, and the fireplaces lit up in gold flames. Out walked two students from the fireplace to the left—vampires, and they seemed nervous.

"Welcome!" everyone chorused. They smiled. "Hi," they said back. Their mentors, fellow vampires, greeted them.

The new kids were Chad and Valerie, and they were twins. Valerie had pale skin, golden eyes, and curly red hair to her shoulders. Chad had pale skin, golden eyes, and red hair as well.

Moments later, Lional stepped back in the room, and the vortex disappeared along with the gold flames, and the orb went in his pocket. "Everybody get to say hello?"

"Yes."

"Right, well, welcome to the academy. I'm so glad to have you all here. This year's gonna be amazing! Now let's get to dinner." With that, everyone walked back up and out of the dungeons. "Oh, Chad and Valerie," called the headmaster, "your luggage will be taken to your rooms, and after dinner—your breakfast—you'll get to unpack for a little bit before we go outside." They nodded to show they heard him.

They approached the dining hall and walked in. "Find your seats, please, everyone!" yelled the headmaster. He'd magically magnified his voice somehow, so it was loud enough for all to hear.

"There's a table," said Rachel. They walked over and sat down. It was Everlee, Sandy, Rachel, Lacey, Dametri, Kyle, and two guys that they didn't know.

"Hey," said Dametri, "these are two of my friends, Kevin and Monty. They waved. Kevin and Monty were dwarfs. Suddenly, a bell chimed, and everyone turned to the front.

"Welcome back to our seasoned students, and welcome to our new students," said the headmaster. "Now before we begin, the rules here are as follows: no leaving the school grounds, curfew is at ten o'clock, and there is no fighting unless it's in training for learning purposes. Also, new students, we will be finding your familiars tonight, along with your abilities." He grinned. "Now let's eat." He sat down, and everyone got up, went, and lined up for dinner.

Chapter 6

Familiars and Abilities

Part 1

Later that night, after dinner, Evie and Sandy were in their room, relaxing and looking at the new school supplies that they got. They had gone to the school supplies room with the other first years, the mentors, and the headmaster, and they all got to pick out a shoulder bag, two leather-bound notebooks, a few scrolls, two ink containers, and two feather quill pens, and they were told that when they ran low, they could come back and get more. Sandy had picked out a purple bag, and Evie picked out a black one. Suddenly, there was a knock on the door.

"Come in," called Sandy, and in walked Lacey and Rachel.

"It's time to get going," said Rachel, and so off they went with Everlee locking the door behind them.

They made their way down the hall. "What's a familiar?" Sandy piped up suddenly.

"It's a protector, a spirit that has taken the form of an animal, a guide, and a friend. You'll take care of each other. Now not all animals are familiars though, but they can be different animals, like cats, dogs, horses, owls—different animals. The headmaster has a hawk called Arden. There was a dragon once, two hundred years ago I heard, but no one has had one since."

"Why not?" asked Everlee.

"They're rare."

"When's the last time you saw a dragon? And you'd have to be very special to get one," said Lacey.

Everlee remembered that her dad had a dog and her mom had an owl. *Their familiars,* she thought.

They made their way outside. They walked outside, and up above them were balls of light floating as lighting and a guide to follow. The sky was full of stars; the air, ripe with the scent of flowers. They reached the waterfall. There were chairs lined in a half circle by the body of water beneath the waterfall, and the light from the castle was illuminating as well. The students were all coming out and sitting down, and now that Evie knew what familiars were, she wasn't too surprised to see a bunch of animals by the students. She'd seen some animals inside today too.

Rachel led them to the water's edge. There stood the other mentors and the other eight first years.

"Headmaster Lional should be here soon," said Lacey.

"Do your familiars have to be with you all the time?" asked Sandy.

"No," said Lacey, "you don't have to be next to each other all the time. They'll come if you call them if you're in danger. Sometimes they go and do their own thing, but if so, they aren't gone long, and there's a bond between you."

"That's so cool," Sandy said. Everlee thought so too, and she wondered what she would get. What if no familiar picked her?

"Has anyone ever not been bonded with a familiar?" Everlee asked Rachel.

"No." Rachel smiled. "It has never happened. It's okay, Evie, don't worry. It'll be okay, you'll see."

Evie nodded. She hoped so.

A few minutes later, everyone was seated, and Everlee and her friends, along with the rest of the mentors and the first years, sat on the ground on the edge of the water. Headmaster Lional approached while the other teachers sat to the side of the student body.

Headmaster Lional spoke, "Welcome, everyone, to the ceremony. Let us first begin with the abilities portion before moving on to the familiars." He grinned. "The first test is water. First years, turn around and stand facing the water. Clear your head, spread out five feet apart along the water, and close your eyes. Focus on the water and picture it rising. Now slowly lift your hands up above your head. If you have the gift, when I tell you to open your eyes, you'll see the water has risen up in front of you. It may not be as risen up as the others, but that's okay."

Everlee closed her eyes and pictured the water rising up higher and higher as she lifted her arms up above her; she heard some students gasp. Then Headmaster Lional spoke, "Now, first years, open your eyes."

Everlee opened her eyes and gasped too. The water in front of her was the highest; it was ten feet high, and out of the other first years, only hers, Kyle's, and Sandy's were raised.

"Three water talents, lovely!" said Lional. "Now the wind. First years, turn and face me." They turned, and a vampire teacher came forward and placed ten small pillows before them. "First years, focus on your pillows, imagine a gust of wind moving them in some way, and then move your hands in the way you want them to move."

Everlee looked at the pillow and closed her eyes. She pictured it spinning. She lifted her left hand up, and with the right hand, she twirled her finger in circles.

"Open your eyes, please."

Everlee opened her eyes, and before her was her pillow, spinning in the air just like it was in her head, and Grace's pillow had apparently flew and hit a third-year guy in the face. *Whoops! Well, at least they're soft,* Evie thought. She also saw Sandy's and Jack's pillows raised too, along with Chad's and Valerie's.

"Six wind talents, wonderful! Next, earth. Mentors, please put the pots of soil before your first years." The mentors got up, went to the left, and grabbed the pots. Rachel put hers in front of Evie and smiled. "Good luck," she said. Evie gave a nervous smile.

"Now, there's so much we could do, but tonight, I want you to make a flower grow. The same concepts apply, only this time, close your eyes and put your hands on the soil while you picture your flower."

Everyone closed their eyes. Everlee pictured her mother's roses, and suddenly, she could feel something coming out and grazing her hands.

"Open your eyes," Lional called.

Everlee already knew. She opened her eyes, and in her pot was the start of a rose bush with little roses on it. Kyle had grown a sunflower; Hannah and Aiden both grew tulips.

"Four earth talents, superb! Now there are three tests left, one of which hasn't been seen in two hundred years, so don't worry if no one gets it later," the headmaster said. They all nodded. "Now then, the fire test. Turn around and face the waterfall." They did. "Now this time, close your eyes, picture a ball of fire in your hands, and when you have it, hold your hands like you're holding a ball and push your hand out like you're pushing it toward the waterfall—and begin."

Everlee pictured it. Suddenly, she could feel the heat in her hands, but it didn't hurt. She pushed her hands in the direction of the waterfall.

"Open your eyes," called the headmaster.

Everlee opened her eyes and saw four fireballs hit the waterfall and extinguish. One was hers; she'd felt it and saw it flying out from her direction. The others were Robert's, Chad's, and Valerie's.

"Four fire talents, that's great!" Lional exclaimed, smiling. "Now the last two test will take place in the open field. Everyone, let us make our way there, and mentors, lead your first years."

With that, Everlee and her friends, along with everybody else, made the walk over to the open field of wildflowers she had seen earlier. The balls of light floating above them guided them and provided them with the vison to see in the dark. It was beautiful.

Evie was in shock. Four talents and two more tests to go. She couldn't believe it. Would she have the other two as well? Was it possible?

Chapter 7

Familiars and Abilities

Part 2

They made their way into the field of wildflowers. There were more balls of light right above the field. All the teachers and students went to the right edge of the field, and the mentors and first years all followed Headmaster Lional to the left side.

"Now, first years," Lional began, "the next test is weather. Not many have it, so if you don't, that's okay. These last two tests, we're gonna do individually. Now, Sandy, you first."

Sandy stepped forward and went over to the spot Lional had pointed to, about twenty feet out in the field, next to a red flag. Evie could see she was nervous. *You can do this,* Evie thought.

"Now," Lional spoke out, "I want you to keep your eyes open. Weather is one of the hard ones to test. I want you to think of a sad memory, something that really upset you, and we'll see what comes." He smiled.

Everlee whispered to Lacey, "So weather isn't a common gift?"

"No," she replied, "not many have it." Evie nodded to show she'd heard.

Everyone was watching Sandy. Everlee could see her face go sad; she looked like she wanted to cry. Suddenly, it started to rain above her, and her eyes went all purple.

"Excellent!" beamed Lional, clapping his hands. "We have a weather talent!" Lional exclaimed, and Lacey pulled a blanket out from a bag that had been there when they arrived. "Here," Lacey said to Sandy, draping it over her, "dry off."

"Thanks," Sandy said. Her eyes weren't purple anymore. *The eyes must only go purple when you're using it,* Evie thought.

"You did wonderful!" Evie said to her, smiling. Sandy hugged her and smiled back. Evie stood there and watched as one by one, her fellow peers all went out and came back—no one else had been able to do it—until it was just her left to go try. *Wow,* she thought, *maybe Sandy is the only weather talent in our group.*

"Everlee, your turn, my dear," called Headmaster Lional. Evie stepped forward over to the same spot as everyone else had. "Now, Everlee, think of a sad memory."

Everlee pictured the day she had learned that she would be leaving her family and Sandy behind, before she found out Sandy was coming, and how she had felt so scared and sad. Next thing Everlee knew, it was raining over her.

"Well done!" she heard Lional call out. "Another weather talent!"

She went back, and Rachel handed her a blanket. "You were so good," Rachel said.

"Yes, you were," said Sandy and Lacey too.

Everlee smiled back. "Thanks," she said. She caught Dametri smiling at her, too, and felt a blush coming on before she turned back to look at the headmaster.

"The last test before we find your familiars is regeneration. Now while weather is not a common gift, regeneration is very rare. We haven't had a student with this gift in two hundred years. Nevertheless, we will test. But first, a little about the gift—you can heal animals and people with it, but when they are to injured and far gone, you can't. To do so would be wrong and cursing them to live on in pain, understood?" he asked. They all nodded. "Very well," he said, "now if you do have the gift, you will be studying with me once a week. I don't have it, but as headmaster, I'm the best one to teach you, and I have information on it as well so that I can help you. Now, Rachel, please take our injured friend out from the basket."

Behind the bag with blankets was a basket. Rachel reached in and pulled out a dove; its wing was broken. *Poor thing,* thought Everlee.

"Now, first years, Rachel will come to each of you, and you will put your hands on the bird that she's holding and think of taking the dove's pain away, imagine the wing healing."

Everlee watched as one by one, everyone failed to heal the poor bird till finally Rachel stood in front of her. "Your turn, Evie," said Rachel. Evie put her hands on the dove's wing and stared into its eyes. *The poor thing,* she thought, *how I wish I could take away your pain.* That's all that Evie thought—taking the pain away and the bird's wing healing.

Suddenly, her hands felt tingly, and the bird got up from lying down; its wing was healed! It looked at her as if to say thanks and then flew off. Suddenly, everyone was clapping and cheering.

"Well done! Well done indeed!" exclaimed the headmaster. "Our first regeneration talent in two hundred years! I look forward to working with you." He smiled. Evie smiled too but more of a shocked smile. *Wow,* she thought, *I have all the talents, and the fact that I'm the only regeneration talent in two hundred years—just wow!*

"All right, settle down!" called the headmaster. After a few minutes, everyone was quiet. "Now it's time for the familiars." He smiled. "Mentors, please take your first years out to the middle of the field and sit down next to them and form a semicircle. I want a mentor between each first year, and I'll be right there."

Everlee and the rest of the first years and mentors went out and did just that, with Lacey on her left and Rachel on her right. Sandy was on the other side of Lacey.

Lional came up. "Mentors, please call your familiars." They did. Suddenly, a slew of names was called out.

Rachel's came first, a red fox. "This is Jasper," she said.

"He's very sweet." Evie petted him.

Lacey had a black squirrel named Tucker, and Dametri had a ferret named Sasha. Everlee looked around at the familiars. There was a variety.

"Now," said Lional, "take these crystals and hold them. Clear your mind, feel your powers flow through you, your energy, and mentally call out to your familiar. Tell them that you're waiting and ready."

Evie took her crystal, and once everyone else had theirs, they closed their eyes. After a while, Lional instructed them to open their eyes. Evie looked down. Her crystal and the others' were glowing.

"Now, mentors, if you could have your familiars take these to the sacred spot and bring the familiars back here to claim their person, we'll wait."

Rachel told Evie to give Jasper the crystal. He took it in his mouth, and the familiars walked off til they couldn't see them anymore. While they waited, Rachel told Everlee how their familiars will be in the form of a baby animal, which they will raise and bond with. "These spirits are new, but they are powerful."

After some time had passed, the familiars started coming back. Dametri's familiar, Sasha, walked up to Kyle with a baby sugar glider on its back. *Awww,* Evie thought.

"It's a girl," said Kyle, holding her to his chest.

"Well, name her," said Dametri.

"Okay, I'll call her Kiki."

Suddenly, Tucker came up to Sandy carrying a tiny egg. She held it, and once hatched, it revealed a baby owl. It was a beautiful gray-and-white owl, a great gray owl. Sandy held the baby owl. "I feel like it's a boy," she said. "I'll call him Cyrus."

"He's so sweet," Evie said.

Then Chad and Valerie had their familiars. Chad got a small egg too, which hatched into a tiny red thing. "Headmaster Lional!" Chad yelled. "What is it? Did I break it?" he asked, looking concerned.

"No, my boy, that is a baby raven. They aren't born with feathers, but they grow them."

Chad looked down and nodded. "I feel better now," he said. He held it close, and after a moment, he announced that it was a boy and called him Midnight. Valerie got a raccoon baby and named her Sable.

Evie looked around. Nearly everyone had their familiars. After a few minutes had passed, everyone else had a familiar—Hannah had a baby lemur, Grace had a baby cheetah, Jack had a baby eagle, Robert had a baby lion, and finally, Aiden had a baby moose. She was the only one without one, and Jasper was still gone.

"Rachel . . ." Evie started.

"It's okay, Evie," Rachel said. "Jasper will bring your companion." Evie nodded. Now everyone was staring at Evie and looking out for Jasper. Suddenly, Jasper came back rolling a big, blue-speckled egg with his nose. He rolled it up to Evie and went to Rachel, who proceeded to pet him.

"What is it?" Evie asked out loud.

"That is a dragon's egg, I do believe," said Lional, coming over and kneeling down by her. "I can't believe it. We haven't had a dragon in two hundred years. You're very lucky, my dear girl." He smiled.

Evie was in shock. *Me. I was chosen to bond with a dragon!* "Well, do I wait for it to hatch?"

"I don't think you'll have to. Look down," he said.

She did, and suddenly noticed that the egg was hatching. It was cracking, and everyone watched. After a few minutes, the top fell off, and there was this little baby dragon, a silvery baby-blue–colored one with a black upside-down triangle around its right eye. With beautiful, piercing gold eyes, it stared up at her. She reached down and picked it up; she could just feel that it was a boy. "It's a boy," she said. She brought him up by her face and looked into his eyes.

"Hello, Oreck." She smiled at him.

Chapter 8

After the Ceremony

Everlee and the rest of the first years were told how they would feed and care for their familiars. Each was given a book on what to feed them and how to care for them. "Now, don't forget to follow your gut too," said Lional as he gave Evie a book on dragons. "I brought this just in case. Now, first years and mentors, we'll stop by the cafeteria before you head to bed to grab some food for them for tonight. Classes begin at eight in the morning, except for you two, Chad and Valerie. The vampire students start classes in a little bit. You will, of course, get a little bit of time to feed and spend with your familiars before the mentors come to take you to your first class.

"All right, everyone," Lional spoke magically, projecting his voice again, "time to go inside, and remember, curfew is in forty minutes, then everyone to your rooms for the night. Unless, of course, you're a vampire student. First years and mentors, follow me. These little ones must be hungry. We'll grab them food, and then you'll take them to your rooms and feed them and go to bed."

Evie nodded, and with that, they made their way to the dining hall, Evie holding Oreck close along the way. Everyone kept looking at her and whispering, looking at her in awe, and some even shouted to her that they liked her dragon.

They finally got to the dining hall, and Headmaster Lional led them to the kitchen in the back. "Mentors, please help the first years get some food for their familiars. We have a special area for food for a variety of familiars, and you may grab your own a treat for helping tonight."

Rachel helped Evie grab Oreck food and grabbed Jasper a treat too. A few minutes later, they left the dining hall and made their separate ways to their rooms for the night.

"Good night!" chorused Rachel and Lacey.

"'Night!" chorused Sandy and Evie back before heading inside and closing the door.

"Oreck and Cyrus are gonna be great friends too, just like us," said Sandy.

"Yes, I do think they will," said Evie as they sat down and fed them.

A few minutes later, they finished up and got ready for bed. Sandy lay down with Cyrus. "Good night," she said.

"Good night," said Evie, rolling over, and Oreck snuggled up to her as they fell to sleep.

The next morning, they got up and went down to breakfast with Lacey and Rachel, along with their familiars. Evie was holding Oreck up to her stomach.

"He is so amazing," said Rachel. "I never thought I'd actually get to see a dragon."

"Thanks," Evie said. "He is so amazing." She felt this rush of love for him already. She had only had him for one night and already she could feel the bond. They made it to the dining hall and proceeded to eat breakfast. "What's our first class?" Evie asked, still sitting at the table while feeding Oreck a bottle with a mixture of blood and goat's milk since he wasn't on solid foods yet. But before Rachel could respond, a teacher Evie could only assume came up and spoke. She was in her midthirties, a black woman with green eyes and curly brown hair to her shoulders.

"Hello," she said, "I'm Ms. Perdy, I'll be teaching you and the other first years—minus the vampire students—this morning. They already had classes and are off to bed. Mentors, please bring them to my classroom in twenty minutes, then you can go to your classes and come back after first period to take them to their second-period class. They will get their schedules from me. Don't worry if you're late, the other teachers know you're helping today." With that, she walked off.

Rachel spoke up, "Well, there's your answer." She grinned. Evie nodded to show she was listening. The girls all walked together to Ms. Perdy's classroom number 313; it was on the third floor. When they reached the classroom, Evie was about to go in with Sandy and the others when, suddenly, Dametri stopped her.

"Hey, Everlee," he said.

"Hey, Dametri," she replied.

"You were amazing last night, you know. I've never seen someone with all the talents."

"Thanks," she said, trying not to blush.

"May I pet him?" he asked, gesturing to Oreck.

"Sure," she said.

Dametri reached down and let Oreck smell his hand before petting him. "He's so cool. Hey, little guy." Oreck seemed to like him too. "Well, I better go, bye," he said, waving before heading off.

"Bye." She waved back before heading inside.

A few moments later, a bell chimed. "All right, class, my name is Ms. Perdy, and I'm the second in command here. I will be making your schedules and seeing if any of you would like to try out for the warriors, and then we'll go from there." Suddenly, a red salamander walked across her desk, making Hannah and Grace gasp. "It's all right, girls, that's my familiar. He won't harm you. His name is Clyde.

"Now, class, the warriors are protectors. They will take girls and boys. Now let me be clear—there's no special treatment. Everyone gets the same test, and no slacking just because you're a girl. Now before I make the schedules, how many would like to try out so I can schedule it this week for you? Bear in mind, vampires can join too. They would be on the night division. Anyone can try, but hear this, not everyone will make it, and there's no shame if you don't. It's hard and elite for a reason—the warriors need to be the best."

Evie raised her hand. "I'd like to try out," she heard herself say. Everyone looked at her, and Ms. Perdy had a sliver of a grin on her face.

"Very well, Ms. Jamison (Everlee's last name, although not used often)."

Evie looked down at Oreck to avoid the gaze of her peers. Oreck's eyes met hers, and she felt a calmness; it was like he was looking into her soul. She knew he believed in her. "Thanks, Oreck," she whispered as she stroked his head.

Jack, Robert, and Aiden decided to try out as well. Ms. Perdy made up their schedules and passed them out. Everlee and Sandy looked at the schedules. The girls had water, wind, and weather classes together, and Everlee had regeneration class Saturday after breakfast with the headmaster. She was also taking earth and fire classes. All classes were for beginners, which was what they were. Everlee also saw that Saturday after lunch was the warrior tryouts. Five classes a day, Monday through Friday, with sixth period for meditation, Saturdays after breakfast with the headmaster, and Sundays off to relax. Everlee definitely had the most classes, but those with less than three talents had classes for twice as long, and everyone except Evie had fitness class—at least Evie didn't have fitness. Also everyone was to take meditation at the end of the day during sixth period. Ms. Perdy also informed them that the academy had a sick bay for injuries and sickness.

The class spent the rest of the time talking about their schedules and warriors, and then a kitchen staff named Ms. Poppy suddenly came in. She was in her thirties as well, with curly blond hair to her shoulders and hazel eyes. She gave them all more food for their familiars. "Those babies have got to eat," she said, smiling.

"Very well, let's take the rest of the class time to feed those babies, and for those with fire talents, I will teach the first years, so all other classes, follow your schedules, and Fire Class 101 starts right here tomorrow after breakfast."

After a few minutes, the familiars were fed, and they were cleaned up, because some went to the bathroom. Moments later, the bell chimed.

Sandy spoke up, "Let's go, Evie, time for Weather 101." She smiled, and Evie nodded. They went out the hall, met Rachel and Lacey, and with that, were off to class.

Chapter 9

Classes

Everlee, Sandy, Rachel, and Lacey all walked to weather class. It was on the first floor in a room just off to the side of the back door to go outside room 108.

"Bye, girls, see you after," chorused Rachel and Lacey.

"Bye," Sandy and Everlee chorused back before heading inside. They went inside and sat down in the front, and moments later, their teacher came in. He was in his early twenties. He had black hair to his shoulders, which were tucked behind his ears, clear muscles in his arms, and blue eyes.

"Welcome, girls. I'm your teacher for Weather 101. My name is Mr. Jones. I'm the headmaster's son." He looked at a paper in his hand. "So just the two of you, eh?" They nodded. "Awesome," he replied. "Well, as I'm sure you realized, not everyone has weather—it's not a common gift. We'll be learning how to summon and control the weather with different emotions, not just using sad memories but also with our wills, willing it and wanting it enough to happen."

They looked at each other and smiled.

"Now, who is Sandy, and who is Everlee?" he asked.

"I am Everlee, sir," Evie said, raising her hand.

He smiled. "And you must be Sandy," he said, grinning at Sandy.

"Yes, sir," she said.

"All right then, let's get started."

"Oh, excuse me, sir," piped up Sandy.

"Yes?" he said.

"If I may, where's your familiar?"

He chuckled. "He's over at the waterfall, I imagine." When he saw her confused look, he continued, "His name is Jaws, and he's an alligator. But don't worry, he doesn't hurt the students and staff. Familiars can sense each other and don't normally hurt each other, unless they're protecting their companion and have to.

"Now, Sandy, you go first. I have a little bed in the corner by my desk, just in case we have any students with baby familiars. You can put your little guy—uh, girl?—in it."

"It's a boy," she said. "His name's Cyrus."

"Well, hello, Cyrus," he said, reaching out and stroking him softly. Sandy put Cyrus on the little bed, then walked over to Mr. Jones. "Now I want you to just let your mind wander, see where it goes, close your eyes, and get lost in it. Allow your emotions to come out and surround you." He stepped back, and they watched. She was smiling; it must be a happy thought. Suddenly, it felt like a rush of warmth swept over the room. "Very good!" Mr. Jones exclaimed, clapping. "The warmth was lovely. Now please take your seat. Everlee, your turn."

Evie put Oreck by Cyrus. "I'll be right here," she told him and went to stand where Sandy had just been. She closed her eyes and felt her mind start to churn in thought. She was a little girl, maybe seven, running through the castle, playing tag with her mother and Sandy. Suddenly, Mr. Jones clapped.

"Try to keep that thought, but open your eyes and look up." She did. Above her head was a cloud with a small rainbow coming out of it.

Sandy exclaimed, "That's so pretty, Evie!"

"I don't see many rainbows in people's first class. Well done to you both. All right now, I'm gonna pass out a book on how our will and emotions influence the weather. Please read the first two chapters."

A little while later, the bell chimed. "See you girls tomorrow," called Mr. Jones.

"Bye," they chorused.

Rachel and Lacey were waiting outside. "Where to next?" asked Rachel.

"I got wind," Sandy said.

"Me too," said Evie.

"Perfect. Okay, let's go," said Lacey. They went to another classroom on the first floor, this one by the front door off to the side down a little hallway, room 103. Grace and Jack were there a few minutes later too. "Well, bye, girls," chorused Rachel and Lacey.

"Bye." They waved.

"Hey, Evie. Hi, Sandy," said Grace and Jack.

"Hi," they said, and they went in and took their seats. The window was opened, and there was a perch by the desk. On the perch was a hummingbird, a little green-and-blue one.

"Aww," said Sandy. Cyrus gave a little noise. "Oh, it's okay, you're my favorite," she said, smiling at him and stroking him; he looked happy.

In walked a woman in her early twenties with light-brown hair to the middle of her back and green eyes.

"Hello, class, I am your teacher, Ms. Love, and this is my familiar. Her name is Cleo."

Suddenly, Cleo took off out the window. Ms. Love chuckled. "She's off to go do her thing and find some flowers. She'll be back. Now, who is who?" So they went around and introduced themselves and their familiars. "I'm so glad to meet you all." She smiled. "All right, now I know some teachers practice first and then have you read. I'm gonna have you read first, then we'll practice, okay?" They nodded. She passed out the books to them. "Okay, please read the first two chapters."

A little bit later, they were all done and waiting for her to give instructions. "Okay, all done?" They nodded. "Okay, let's begin." Then she gave everybody a bowl of sand and told them, "Now don't touch it. Use your mind, only remember what the book said about willing it. I want you to imagine a strong wind rushing over the sand, sending it flying in the air."

They tried and tried, but so far, Evie was the only one to make her sand rise. Finally, after some time, everyone's sand started to move in the air.

"Now imagine a huge gust of wind blowing it out the window." They did, and a gust so strong blew through the classroom, sending most of the sand out the window. "Excellent!" Ms. Love clapped; she seemed pleased. Suddenly, the bell chimed. "All right, class, I'll see you tomorrow."

They went out, and waiting there was Rachel and Lacey. They went to lunch, fed their familiars, and went to the bathroom. "Now where to?" Lacey asked.

"Water," they chorused.

"Okay, let's go," said Rachel. They went to the second floor room 203 and parted ways.

They went inside and took their seats. Moments later, Kyle walked in. "Hey, girls" he said.

"Hi," they chorused back.

He sat next to Sandy when in walked their teacher. She was in her midthirties with curly black hair and brown Asian eyes. "Hello, class. Welcome to Water 101. I am Ms. Hong."

"Where's you familiar?" asked Kyle, raising his hand.

She smiled. "My familiar's an otter. He's hanging out right now by the waterfall. His name's Miles. Now, everybody, gather 'round." She yanked a big bowl out of the closet, set it on an empty desk, and filled it with water. "Now, everybody, cup your hands over the bowl, picture the water rising and filling your hands. Let your desire flow through you." They stood there, and after a few minutes, the water filled their hands. "Well done," she said. "All right, you may take your seats." She passed out books. "Please read the first two chapters." A little while later, the bell chimed. "I'll see you tomorrow," she called. They waved goodbye.

Dametri, Rachel, and Lacey were waiting. "Now where?" asked Lacey.

"I have fitness," said Sandy.

"Okay, let's go." And the girls took off.

"And what about you?" Rachel asked Evie.

"Earth," Evie said.

"Me too," said Kyle.

"Well then, let's go," said Dametri. He took them down the hall to room 212.

"See you," said Rachel. Evie waved.

"Bye, man," said Kyle.

Dametri nodded. "Bye, Evie," said Dametri. "You have fun, okay?" She smiled. "Thanks," she said.

He took off, and Evie went inside. Moments later, Aiden and Hannah joined them. Suddenly, their teacher, a man in his early forties with shaggy brown hair and brown eyes came in. "Hello, class. I'm Mr. Adams, and this," he said, pulling a tarantula out of his pocket and setting it on his desk, "is Hudson. He's my familiar, and he won't hurt you. Now introductions." So they went around saying their names. "Okay, now books," he said. He was rambling in the closet and came out with the books. "Here, please pass these around," he said, handing them to Kyle, so he did. "Now read the first two chapters, please."

A little bit later, Mr. Hudson said they were going to go down and go outside in the back, so they followed him downstairs and outside. They went over to the garden. He led them inside the fenced area.

"Now, everyone, come over here. This row hasn't fully grown yet. They're tomatoes. Everyone, kneel down and place your hands over the earth. Imagine the tomato seeds sprouting and growing." Evie and the others did just that. Hannah and Aiden produced a few sproutlings; Kyle grew two tomatoes on his small plant, and Everlee's fully blossomed with a bunch of medium-sized tomatoes.

"Well done," Mr. Adams said, clapping.

The bell chimed, and Oreck made cooing noise at Evie and tipped his head before nuzzling her, as if to say "Good job." She petted him. "Thanks, Oreck," she said.

"All right, everyone, I'll see you tomorrow in the classroom. Have a good day!"

Rachel and Dametri came over to take Kyle and Evie to meditation class.

"How was class?" Rachel asked.

"It was great," said Kyle.

"Meditation is by the waterfall," said Dametri. "At least until it gets cold out, then it'll be moved indoors."

"All right, well, see you guys later," said Rachel after they had gotten to the waterfall.

"Bye," said Evie.

Suddenly, Kyle shouted, "Hey, Sandy!"

Evie turned. Sure enough, Sandy was headed their way. Lacey waved goodbye since Sandy had spotted them. A few moments later, the rest of the first years arrived. Then a woman in her thirties with red hair to her shoulders and blue eyes came up.

"Hello, I'm your teacher, Ms. Bell, and that," she said, pointing to the side of the garden to a big deer with big antlers, "is my familiar. His name is Casper."

They spent the class introducing themselves and their familiars to Ms. Bell. She seemed shocked, but in a good way, to see a dragon. She smiled at Oreck. Then they lay down and looked up at the sky. "Close your eyes, clear your heads, and now let your minds wander."

It was very calm. Evie liked this class. Well, she liked them all, but still.

A while later, the bell chimed. "See you tomorrow, everybody!" called Ms. Bell. They all waved and chorused goodbye to her before heading inside for the night.

It had been a good first day of class, and Evie had fire class the next day.

The next morning, Everlee went to fire class. Ms. Perdy had them read two chapters and then held a candle and try to light it with their minds. Evie was the only one that could do it. Robert's flickered then went out. "That's all right," said Ms. Perdy. "It's only day one. Good job." Then the bell chimed, and Evie went to the rest of her classes, and by the end of the day, she was so tired, but it had been another good day.

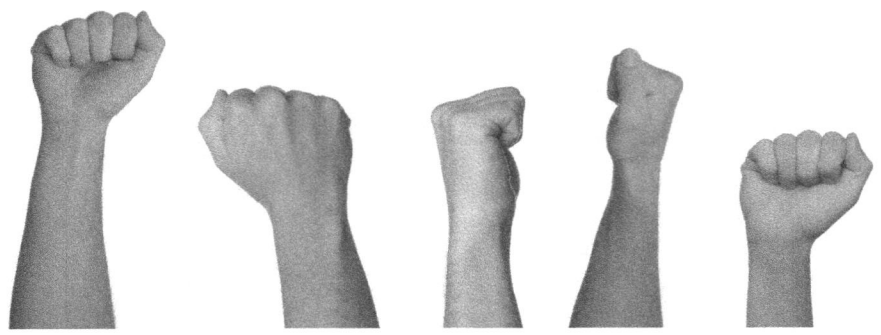

Chapter 10

Regeneration with the Headmaster and Warrior Tryouts

Everlee woke up that morning. She and Sandy got dressed and went down to the dining hall for breakfast with Oreck and Cyrus. Oreck was sitting on her shoulder; he'd just started doing that a few days ago. Everlee reflected on their first week of classes; it had gone by fast.

They got to the dining hall, got in line, and got their food—pancakes and bacon and a bottle for Oreck and some food for Cyrus. They made their way to a table, and minutes later, they were joined by Kyle, Dametri, Rachel, Lacey, Grace, and Hannah. Everyone was having a grand time talking. Suddenly, Evie stood up. "I'm gonna throw my food away. Oreck and I have class with the headmaster. I hope I do okay."

"Good luck," everyone chorused. Evie waved, threw her food away, and left the dining hall. Halfway down the hall, she heard "Hey, Evie, wait up!" She turned; it was Dametri.

"Why don't I walk you to his office?"

"That would be nice." She smiled at him.

"So I hear you're trying out for the warriors later today," he said. She nodded. "That's great," he said. "I hope you get in. I'm a warrior too. I'll be rooting for you."

"Thanks," she said. A little later, he bid her goodbye at the headmaster's office. "Bye." She waved.

Evie knocked. "Come in," called the headmaster. She opened the door. Lional was next to the window with Arden on his shoulder, seemingly enjoying the view while pondering some thoughts.

"Hello, my dear," he began, "please take a seat." He gestured to a chair by his desk. She took her seat. "Now I'm gonna do my best to teach you. This is new territory, but we'll learn together. I have a book on regeneration. I've already read it, and now I'd like you to read it—a chapter per night, please." She took the book and nodded. "How has classes been?"

"They have been good," she replied.

"Good, I'm glad to hear that," he said. Arden seemed to be studying Oreck, and Oreck, him. "Hello, Oreck," said Lional. "May I?" he asked, stretching his hand toward Oreck.

"Of course," she said.

He stroked Oreck's back. "He is so remarkable. How have you been bonding?" he asked. "Is he eating all right?"

"Good, and yes, he is," she responded.

Lional smiled. "Good, I'm glad," he said, removing his hand. "Now if you don't mind, I thought we'd go to the sick bay and practice a bit."

"Okay," she nodded, and off they went.

The sick bay was on the third floor, at the very end of the hall, just to the right before the stairs. They went in. Evie had never been in the sick bay; it had twenty beds—ten in a row on either side—and a small staircase in the back leading up somewhere. "That's where Nurse Emily resides, and it's also her office It has two rooms." She nodded. There were oil lamps on the night tables in between the beds, and screens were folded in the corner for when needed. There was a cabinet with supplies, except for the medicine that was in her office, and a glass skylight ran the length of the room in a line.

Suddenly, Nurse Emily came down. She was an older woman in her midfifties, with brown hair with some gray in it, and hazel eyes. Walking next to her was a black cat with green eyes. "That is Nurse Emily," said Lional, "and her familiar. His name is Gizmo. He's a sweet boy that will go around sometimes and cuddle those that aren't feeling well. Students love Gizmo."

"Ah, Headmaster," said Nurse Emily, coming over. "To what do I owe the pleasure?"

"My dear Emily, this is Everlee. She has the gift of regeneration, and I thought she and I could help out here, and she could use her gift."

Nurse Emily looked at Evie, so surprised. "Why, we haven't had a regeneration talent in two hundred years. This is remarkable!"

"Yes, it is," said Lional.

"Well, of course, you may help," said Nurse Emily. "We only have a few. Let's see, I'll find an easy one to start her off. Ahh, over here."

They walked over and, to Evie's horror, found Gertrude and her familiar, a scorpion. *Ugh,* she thought.

"What is she doing here?" asked Gertie.

"Now mind your manners, young lady." Gertie looked sore at that. "She's going to help you. Ms. Gertrude fell this morning and broke her ankle. I was going to give her crutches, but if she will allow it, Ms. Everlee may be able to heal her so there won't be a need."

Everlee looked at Gertie. "May I?" she asked her.

"Fine," said Gertrude. Everlee sat by her and gently laid her hands on Gertie's ankle.

"Ow! Watch it!" said Gertie. Evie fought the urge to tell her to stop whining.

"Now, Everlee, I want you to remember how you felt with the dove, how you wanted to take away its pain."

Evie nodded, closed her eyes, and focused on Gertrude's ankle. *Well, I'll be the bigger person,* Evie thought, and so she thought of taking away Gertrude's pain. After a moment, she felt her hands tingle.

"Hey!" she heard Gertrude exclaim. "My ankle doesn't hurt anymore!"

Evie opened her eyes. Gertie was moving her ankle. Nurse Emily examined it. "Remarkable," she said, and to Evie's shock, Gertie said, "Thank you."

"You're welcome," Evie responded.

"Well, I think that's a good start for day one of class. Remember the first chapter." Evie nodded. "And, Nurse Emily, I take it we can continue coming here?"

"Why, of course." She smiled.

"Very well then, Ms. Everlee, I do believe the bell's going to ring soon for lunch, and you want to eat a good lunch, especially with tryouts today." Suddenly, the bell chimed.

A little bit later, Everlee was on her way to lunch. She made a stop by her room to change into black pants, a black form-fitting top, and black leather gloves for tryouts. She wanted the top tighter so it didn't fly up easily, just in case.

She had made her way to the dining hall and had lunch, a bowl of stew and bread with a glass of milk, and Oreck had a bottle. Soon he would be on solids, and she would also have to teach him to breathe fire.

Evie and her friends made their way outside. "So why was Gertie staring at lunch?" asked Rachel.

"Probably 'cause I healed her ankle. She actually said 'thank you.'" Rachel looked surprised.

They got down to the outdoor training area for the warriors, and minutes later, they were joined by Jack, Robert, and Aiden. They were all good guys, although sometimes Jack was a bit arrogant or confident as he called it.

"Good luck, guys," Evie said.

"You too," they said.

Everlee saw that some chairs had been set out by the training area. "Warriors and first years trying out, please be seated," called the sergeant. "My name is Sergeant Hyde and that"—she gestured to the stable areas; right next to it was a beautiful black horse—"is my familiar. His name is Holt." Sergeant Hyde was a black woman in her midthirties with short black hair, gray eyes, and muscles in her arms. She looked tough. "All but the night sergeant and the night warriors are here. Why? Because we're a team and therefore will be here, should you succeed, to welcome you in." Dametri winked at her. "First up is Robert. Your objective is in two parts. Hold your own as long as possible against a warrior of my choice and complete the obstacle course. Okay now, Robert, you will go up against Rowland."

Rowland stepped forward. He was a third year by the look of him, Asian, with brown hair cut short, brown eyes, and some muscles in his forearms. His familiar, a black lab, stayed where he had stood. Robert and Rowland made their way to the center of the mat.

"On the count of three, you go. Now no shots to the groin, no punching. For tryouts, you will wrestle each other to the ground. To win the match, you must pin your opponent for twenty seconds. Do that, and you move on to part two. Okay, on the ready—three, two, one, go!"

Evie watched as they wrestled. Rowland was good, but Robert was holding his own. Finally, Robert managed to pin Rowland for twenty seconds and was told to go back in line. He would move on to part 2. Aiden went next; he, unfortunately, didn't make it, but not for lack of trying.

"Good try, Aiden," Everlee said.

"Thanks, Evie. It's okay, I tried. I hope you get it." She smiled at him. Then it came time for Jack; he made it.

"All right, last up, Everlee," called the sergeant. Evie handed Oreck to Aiden. "Let's see, you're up against—ah yes, Gertrude."

Gertrude looked at Evie. "Don't expect me to take it easy on you just 'cause you helped me," she said.

"Wasn't planning on it," Evie retorted. Soon they were wrestling. Evie had to admit, Gertie was no weakling, but neither was she. A few moments later, she had Gertie pinned, and Aiden had given back Oreck to her.

"Now, Aiden, I'm sorry, but you must be going. Only warriors and tryouts to phase two, but it was a valiant effort, my boy." Aiden smiled and left.

"Everyone, follow me."

They followed the sergeant and the warriors to one of the unexplored trails next to the field. Halfway down it was an obstacle course. It had logs in a row of ten on the ground, spaced about six inches apart, followed by a maze of zigzagging ropes low to the ground over mud. The only way through was to crawl. A climbing wall came next, followed by three wooden platforms that were spaced five feet apart, which they had to jump to, and lastly, a rope with a bell at the top. The rope was ten feet long and had to be climbed. "Warriors, to the end of the course, please. I'll follow along the side, watching you each try the course."

Evie handed Oreck to Dametri. "I'll keep him safe till you get to the end."

"Thank you." She stroked Oreck's head. "It's okay, I'll be back soon," she said before Dametri walked off.

"Jack, you first," called the sergeant. Everlee and Robert watched him go. He was struggling a bit, but he did it. "Well done!" boomed Sergeant Hyde. "Welcome to the warriors." Jack was smiling from ear to ear, and Evie heard the warriors clapping.

"Now, Robert, you next." Robert was doing well; unfortunately, he fell halfway up the rope at the end. "I'm sorry, my dear boy, but you did put in a very honorable effort."

Robert was disappointed but took it well. "Bye, Everlee, good luck," he said, then left.

"Your turn, Everlee," the sergeant said. Everlee took off down the course. She went a bit slower in the mud-and-ropes part, so she was able to crawl through. Finally, she made it to the last part of the course—the rope and bell. She was halfway up when she could feel her arms starting to give out, but she pushed through it.

"Come on," she told herself, "show everyone what you're made of!"

A moment later, she rang the bell before sliding down. She heard the sergeant call "Welcome to the warriors!" She heard clapping, and next thing she knew, Dametri was right by her side.

"Well done, Evie, that was excellent!" He handed Oreck back to her.

Later on, Everlee was back in her room, relaxing before dinner. She had taken a bath to wash off the mud. She was now a warrior, and the sergeant had said that warriors have training on Saturdays, after lunch. She just lay there with Oreck, reminiscing about her day. It had been a great day, and the annoyed look on Gertie's face earlier made her chuckle too.

Chapter 11

Letters

It had been a month since she joined the warriors. Everlee was relaxing in her room with Oreck. It was a Sunday, and Sandy and Cyrus went off a bit earlier to hang out with Kyle and Kiki. She was happy that Sandy was enjoying herself.

Suddenly, a gushing sound came from her fireplace, and out popped a letter addressed to her. It was from her parents. Everlee bent down and picked it up. She sat back in her chair and read:

My dearest Everlee,

We are so sorry we haven't written before now. By no means have we forgotten about you. The headmaster has kept us updated, and we are so pleased to hear that you had all the talents and a dragon to boot. We are so proud and look forward to meeting your little one, Oreck. We were told you named him. We have also been informed that you made the warriors. We are very impressed; however, please stay safe.

Now we know you must have concerns. Last you knew, we were facing a potential war with the wolves. Your father and I have gotten it under control, at least for now, but we are not naive to the possibility that things can turn. For now, we have captured the rogue wolves—while sleeping, of course, due to their strength—and have warned the king of the consequences. That is all for now. We are still investigating and trying to figure out what's going on.

Please write us back. While we have been updated, there's nothing better than hearing from you, even if it's something funny. We love you so very much.

Sincerely,
Mom and Dad.

PS: Sandy's mother will be sending her a letter soon, if you can let her know. Thanks, darling.

Suddenly, two more letters came out of the fireplace, one for Sandy from her mother. Everlee placed it on Sandy's pillow. The other was addressed to them both, from the headmaster. Inside, it read:

Hello, girls,

The mail comes and goes through your own fireplaces. Don't worry if you have a fire going. It won't burn your mail; it's protected. Hoping all is well.

Take care,
Headmaster Lional.

Evie went to the desk, pulled out paper and an envelope, and started a letter to her parents. She thought she would tell them how things have been going and some funny stuff too.

Dear Mom and Dad,

I was so happy to hear from you! Things are going well. I've made some friends, and one's a boy. His name's Dametri. He's a werewolf, Sir Edgar's younger son. Don't worry though, he's a good guy. He was terribly upset to hear the rumors about what the wolves were doing, and my familiar—his name is Oreck, a dragon like you have heard—is doing well. We have really bonded. He's growing. He's on solids now, and I taught him to breathe fire. The first time he breathed fire, he accidentally burned a good size patch of grass, but I fixed it. Everyone thinks he is amazing.

This boy Chad, in my group, is a vampire. Well, a few weeks ago, he came running through the dining hall at dinner, screaming out "Headmaster Lional!" causing everyone to, of course, turn and watch. He reached the headmaster and was telling him, "Sir, I think my bird's broken!" And in turn, the headmaster took the bird, looked at him, and gave the bird back while telling Chad with a grin, "No, my dear boy, he's not broken; he's just an albino raven." Chad was stunned and stuttered out, "But, sir, he is named Midnight." "I know, talk about the irony. Don't worry, dear boy, he's a fine bird," the headmaster told him. Chad has since come to grips with his white raven; they love each other.

We also have a cook called Ms. Poppy. She's so clumsy, but she's hilarious. Also, I am roommates with Sandy; it is so much fun! And there's this girl Gertrude, she isn't too fond of me, but I think it's because she's jealous. She is a wolf too. I found out when she joined the other wolf students to go down into the holding area during last month's full moon. She doesn't like that Dametri gives me attention. Don't worry, Mom and Dad, you will like him.

The warrior thing is doing good. I usually wake up sore on Sundays, but that's okay.

I'm happy to hear things are okay with the wolves for now, and hopefully, things stay calm.

I love you both so much and miss you both.

Signed with love,
Everlee

Everlee sealed the envelope, took it to the fireplace, and stuck it in (the fire was off); and moments later, it got sucked out of her hands and disappeared. Minutes later, Sandy came in. "Hey, Sandy, there's a letter for you on your bed, and I left the letter from the headmaster on the desk."

Sandy read her letter and was smiling. "Oh, it's so good to hear from Mom. I miss her." She then read the letter from the headmaster, and then wrote a letter, too, and sent it off up the fireplace. "Did you get a letter too?" she asked.

"Yes," Evie said, "from Mom and Dad. I sent one off just before you got back."

"It's gonna be nice to receive letters now, make us a bit less homesick."

"Yes," agreed Everlee. She told Sandy about the update with the wolves. "But please, keep that between us. I may tell Dametri, but that's it, okay?" Sandy nodded. "So how was your time with Kyle?"

She smiled. "It was great. We went out and lay in the far end of the flower field, watching clouds, talking. Cyrus and Kiki played. Kyle snagged some cookies at breakfast, and we ate those." Evie was happy for Sandy; she deserved this. "So when are you gonna go see Dametri? He was looking for you."

"Oh, I don't know," Evie said.

"Come on, Everlee. He's a good guy."

"I know," she said.

"Well, then, off you go, go hang out with him. He was by the waterfall last I saw." Evie smiled, and she and Oreck took off.

Oreck walked beside her. He'd grown. He still wasn't huge and fully grown though, but he'd grown bigger. He was now the size of a medium dog. They reached the waterfall, and sure enough, there was Dametri.

"Hey, Everlee," he called while running up to her.

"Hey." She smiled. "Listen, can we take a walk?" she asked.

"Sure," he said. They made their way down a trail. She told him, after making sure no one was around, about the update on the wolves. He thanked her for telling him. "I'm sorry things are like this. I promise not all werewolves are like this."

"I know," Everlee said. She hugged him and just stood there. It felt nice to be in his arms.

They spent the rest of the afternoon together. Everlee was happy Sandy had insisted she go and find Dametri. After dinner, he walked her to her room and did something he'd never done before; he kissed her hand before leaving. Evie couldn't hold back the blush this time, and when she went in, she proceeded to tell Sandy about her day. They played with Oreck and Cyrus. Soon after, they started to get ready for bed, but before they did, they had a letter drop out of the fireplace. It seemed to be from the headmaster. It read:

Dear students,

There will be a dance on December 16. Boys ask the girls. A pair of dress and tux makers will be here at the end of the week to take measurements, and since there are so many of you, it will take a little time to make them all. You may pick your colors and styles; it has already been paid for by your parents and, for some of you, an anonymous donation.
Don't be upset your parents didn't tell you. I asked them to keep the surprise, but now you may talk about it.

Good evening,
Headmaster Lional

The girls looked at each other and squealed. "Oh, I hope Kyle asks me to go," Sandy said.

"I'm sure he will."

"And I know Dametri is gonna ask you."

"You think?" said Evie.

"Oh, I know," said Sandy. "He clearly likes you, and you just said he kissed your hand."

Evie blushed. "But what about Gertrude?" Evie said.

"What about her?" said Sandy. "It said 'boys ask,' so it's his choice."

Evie nodded. "That's true."

They finally calmed down and headed to bed for the night. It had been a wonderful day. Evie snuggled up to Oreck and drifted off to sleep.

Chapter 12

Confessions of Feelings

The next morning, at breakfast, all the girls were giggling and whispering. Everlee and Sandy, along with Rachel and Lacey, sat together. They were soon joined by Hannah and Grace. Hannah and Grace were discussing who they wanted to ask them. Lacey was talking to Sandy about her time with Kyle last night and how they thought he would ask her for sure. Everlee noticed Rachel wasn't joining in on the discussion.

"Aren't you excited?" she asked Rachel.

"Oh, of course I am, but I'm not worried about a guy asking me. If someone does, then cool, but if not, I'll still go and have a good time."

Evie smiled at her. Rachel was so pretty and confident. She thought the guys here would have to be nuts to miss that. "Well, I think some guy is gonna ask you. They'd be nuts not to like you."

Rachel smiled. "Thanks, Evie."

Suddenly, Gertie walked past with her crew, talking loudly so Evie could hear—clearly on purpose. "I just have a feeling Dametri will ask me. I'm not worried. He has been smiling a lot at me lately, and with my good looks, why wouldn't he want me?" They dissolved into giggles and walked past and out of earshot.

"Ugh," said the girls at the table, groaning in unison.

"Don't worry," Hannah said to Evie, "I'm sure she's just trying to get to you. Clearly he likes you. If I had to bet, I'd place it on you every time." She smiled at Evie.

"Thanks, Hannah," Evie said, smiling back. She thought so too, even if she couldn't deny Gertie was pretty, but then she remembered it was her hand Dametri had kissed yesterday and how he would pick to spend time with her over Gertie multiple times since she had met him. And that thought comforted her. She was fairly sure he would pick her; the question was *when*? Still, they had over a month. The dance was in December, and it was only October.

Classes passed by, and Everlee was getting better in all of them. Although she sometimes felt a bit drained Saturday nights after doing regeneration and warriors, she was loving it. A few days later, the day before everybody was to meet the suit and dress makers, Everlee was sitting out by the waterfall with Oreck. Classes were over for the day, and she was enjoying the outdoors till dinnertime. Suddenly, she heard footsteps and turned around. Walking toward her was Dametri and his familiar, Sasha. "Hey," she called.

He smiled, and when he finally reached her, he sat down. "So how are you?" he asked her.

She shrugged. "I'm okay, just stuck listening to almost all the girls talk about who they think will ask them to the dance and what they want their dresses to look like, with the exception of Rachel. She's pretty chill. She says she's going to go and have fun whether a boy asks her to go or not. She's so confident."

He smiled. "Yeah, she's cool. I think she'll have a guy ask her though." Everlee raised an eyebrow. He laughed. "Not me, no. I heard that Rowland was thinking of asking her. Remember, he's a warrior?"

She nodded. "He's a good guy from what I know, and if he isn't good to her, she'll put him in his place." He laughed. Evie smiled. "So," she said, "have you asked anybody to go?"

He looked suddenly nervous. "Well, no, I haven't. That's why I came over here. No one has asked you to go yet, have they?"

"No," she said.

He looked happy at that. He then placed his hand on the ground next to her, and suddenly, a small rose bush with beautiful roses sprouted up. He picked one and turned to her. "Everlee, would you do me the honor of accompanying me to the dance? I really like you and would love to take you and perhaps be your boyfriend if you share the same feelings."

She took the rose, a mixture of shock and happiness running through her. "Thank you," she said, "it's so pretty, and yes, I would love to go to the dance with you, and I would definitely love to be your girlfriend."

He smiled so big and ran his fingers along the side of her head through her hair. He leaned in and gently kissed her softly on the lips. For that moment, the whole world stopped. It was everything Everlee had hoped her first kiss would be.

A little while later, at dinner, Everlee was sitting with Dametri, Lacey, Rachel, Rowland, Hannah, Grace, and of course, Kyle and Sandy. Rowland had asked Rachel right after classes ended if she would go to the dance with him. Grace shared that Aiden was taking her; he asked her after breakfast. Lacey, Sandy, and Hannah still didn't have dates, although Sandy didn't seem upset. Everlee had reassured her earlier that Kyle was going to ask her; it was so clear that he liked her. Lacey didn't seem worried.

"I mean, I would like a date, but if not, I'll still have fun." Suddenly, a third-year boy, an elf, approached the table and asked to speak in private with Lacey. Minutes later, she came back alone, all smiles. "Oliver just asked me to the dance," she said.

"Congrats," they all said.

Since it was dinnertime, the vampire students were out too; it was their breakfast time. Valerie approached the table. "Hey," she said.

"Hi," they chorused.

"Hey, Hannah, Chad was wanting to talk to you. He's in the hall." Hannah raised an eyebrow. "He's a bit shy," Valerie continued. Hannah nodded and took off to find Chad. Valerie took Hannah's seat. "Just till she gets back." She grinned.

"Is Chad gonna ask her to the dance?" Grace asked. Valerie nodded.

"Has anyone asked you?" Rachel asked Valerie.

She nodded. "Yesterday, a second-year vampire student. His name is John. He seems nice and cute, so I said yes."

Kyle, meanwhile, whispered something to Sandy, and she smiled and nodded.

"What are you whispering?" Lacey teased with a smile.

"Oh, nothing." Sandy smiled. "You'll find out soon enough."

Everlee was content to listen to everyone's chatter. She was having a great night, and dinner was delicious—pot roast, one of her favorites. Oreck was chilling next to her. She stroked his head. "Wanna go for a walk later?" she asked him, and he made one of his noises to signal yes.

After dinner, she, Dametri, Oreck, and Sasha went for a walk, holding hands. Gertrude spotted them. "Hey, Dametri," she said.

"Hey, Gertie."

"So have you found a date for the dance?" she said, trying to avoid their hand-holding.

"Yes, I asked my lovely girlfriend, Evie," he said, gesturing with his eyes to their hands.

"Ah," she said, "I didn't know you two were dating."

"It's new," he said.

"Well, good for you," she said to him. "I'll see you later."

"Okay, bye, Gertie," he called as she walked off.

Dametri and Everlee walked along a trail lit up by fireflies. They stopped and sat on a bench along the trail, and she laid her head on his shoulder as they watched the moon.

"So what color should I have my tux?" he asked.

Everlee thought about it. "Black," she said, "with blue pieces."

He nodded. "So I can assume you're going to have a black-and-blue dress?" She nodded. "Well, it's getting late, I should walk you back."

On the way back, Oreck flew. He had started that, too, a while ago, and he loved it. "One day, when he's grown, I'd like to ride him," Everlee said.

"I bet you will," Dametri told her.

They arrived at her door. Oreck was still outside, flying, but her window was open so he could come back in. Dametri kissed Everlee good night and took off. She sighed happily and went in her room. Moments later, Sandy came in all giddy.

"Kyle asked me out and to be his girlfriend!" she squealed. Evie was happy for her. "Oh, I love it here," said Sandy.

Evie giggled. "I'm glad," she told her. Just before bed, Oreck flew in. "Had a nice fly?" she asked. He looked happy. "One day, when you're grown, can I ride you?" He laid his head on her knee and looked up. She looked into his eyes and seemed to feel him saying yes. They had a special bond indeed; she could feel him communicate, if that made any sense.

The next day, girls and guys were taken down in groups. Evie looked at the list; she was toward the end of the day, after dinner, with Sandy and the vampire students. That was fine by her. Finally, later that day, after dinner, Everlee and Sandy walked down to the first floor to room 100. Valerie was there already.

"Hey," she called. They waved at her and went over. "Where are your familiars?" she asked them.

"They're outside, flying around," Sandy said.

"Where's yours?" Evie asked.

"Same, she's outside. She'll be back."

"Valerie, Sandy, and Everlee," called an older woman with brown hair in a bun and black glasses. "This way please, girls." They followed her in. "My name is Mrs. Hammond, and these are my daughters." She gestured to two ladies in their twenties. "All right, first thing's first, let's get your measurements."

Each daughter took a girl, and Everlee had Mrs. Hammond take her measurements. After the measurements, she talked to Mrs. Hammond about what her dress should look like. Mrs. Hammond wrote it down by her name and measurements and drew a sketch too.

Shortly after, the girls walked out of the room and went outside to go hang out with their familiars. Valerie was enjoying petting Oreck when the bell rang, signaling the time to head inside.

"Goodbye," they said to Valerie, giving her a hug.

"Bye, see you tomorrow at night." She smiled and walked off to class with Sable in tow. It was off to bed for Everlee and Sandy.

With the windows opened, Evie called to Oreck. "Same for you, Cyrus, don't stay out much longer too." Their familiars gave happy noises to show they heard the girls. Then Everlee and Sandy went inside and to their rooms, talking about the fitting.

"So what color is your dress?" Sandy asked Everlee.

"Black and blue," Everlee said. "And yours?"

"Mine's gonna be a royal purple with silver."

"That sounds pretty."

"Thanks," Sandy grinned.

Minutes later, they were in pajamas. Everlee and Sandy quickly wrote letters and sent them to their parents, telling them about everything new, including their new boyfriends. Shortly after they sent the letters off, Cyrus and Oreck came back. They closed the window and went to bed.

Chapter 13

Learning More Information

It had been two weeks since Everlee and Dametri started dating. Gertrude, of course, was still pretty sore about it and had even taken her aside one day, telling her that Dametri was gonna leave her one day and that she would never fully understand him since she wasn't a wolf. Everlee told Gertrude to get over herself and that she would be informing Dametri, which she did, and he sought Gertie out and set her down, telling her that if she couldn't be nice to his girlfriend, then to stay clear of him too, because he couldn't be friends with someone that didn't treat his girlfriend with respect. Gertie tried to backpedal, but he stopped her. "I'm serious, Gertie. If I hear one more time that you're harassing her, we're done, and the only relationship we'll have is a civil one, as me being your future leader."

Gertie looked at him weird. "Dametri, your older brother is next in line."

"Do you presume to tell me you know what all my family and I discuss?" She stopped. "I'm serious, Gertie, knock this off. If not for me, then for yourself. She is the future queen, and if nothing else, you should respect that," he said before he walked off.

Everlee was on the bench, a new favorite spot of theirs, and had just finished listening to Dametri tell her what had happened. She looked confused. "Dametri, if I may ask, what did you mean 'her future leader' if your older brother's next in line?"

He sighed. "This stays between us," he said. She nodded. "My father wrote to me the other day, stating how he was thinking of passing the clan to me instead of my brother, saying how he was growing concerned and that my brother was acting a bit different and was angry at your parents for imprisoning the rogue wolves and thought I was stupid for dating you. My father has never seen this side of him. Mind you, one of the rogue wolves was my uncle Borris, and he and my brother have always been close. He thinks maybe he's just angry his favorite uncle is locked up, but for now, he is having him stay under watch and never left out of sight, for fear he may do something stupid. My dad confessed that's why he didn't stop the rogue wolves, or at least to everyone else, it seemed he hadn't tried or cared, but that's not true. He was handling it privately and hoping to find out what had happened, especially since his brother, Uncle Borris, seemed to be leading them. He finally realized he couldn't handle it and said he gave the last known coordinates to your parents so they could capture them, on the stipulation that none will be killed.

"So you see, my dad is not a bad man, Evie. He just was trying to keep things private, and now he can't. For now, with my brother out of the picture for the clan leader—at least right now, if not permanently. My sister, Anne—she's my brother's twin—is stepping up and is by Dad's side while I'm gone. This summer, if my brother is deemed worthy, he'll fight with me and our sister. If not, Anne and I will fight for beta, which means whomever wins is the next leader, or alpha, after Dad. She never was a huge fan of Uncle Borris and is distraught by this news. You would really like her, I think."

Everlee nodded. "Thank you for telling me this. Don't worry, it's safe with me, I promise.

"I know," he said, leaning over to kiss her.

The rest of the day was spent out in the flower field with their friends, laughing and having a good time. Two days later, Everlee noticed that Dametri and Gertrude, along with the other wolf students, looked a bit pale and sweaty. It was a full moon tonight, and she felt bad.

They always got a bit sick before the full moon. Tonight, they would go to the holding area. She'd never asked him where it was or what it was like down there; maybe she would later.

Everlee had class with the headmaster that she needed to get to. A few minutes later, she was up at the sick bay. Lately, they had been having classes start there and ended them in his office.

"Hey, Nurse Emily," Evie said to the nurse.

"Good day, my dear." She smiled.

"Is Headmaster Lional in yet?"

"No, dear, not yet, but not to worry, he will be here soon, I imagine. I am still in awe of what you can do."

"Thanks," said Evie. "I'm glad I can help people with it."

Suddenly, Headmaster Lional walked in with Arden on his shoulder like usual. "Hello," he said.

"What have you got for us today?" Nurse Emily asked.

"I want to have Everlee heal two people today instead of one. Let's see how it goes."

"Two?" Nurse Emily and Evie said together.

"Yes," Lional answered, smiling. "I think you can do it, Everlee, my dear."

Everlee nodded. She wished Oreck was with her, but he was flying outside though.

"Let's try something new. We have a student that has come down with the flu over here." They walked over and saw Lacey.

"Lacey," Everlee said, "when did you get sick? I just saw you last night."

"This morning I woke up sick," Lacey said.

"Well, I'll do my best to help you."

"I know you will," Lacey said. She tried to smile but couldn't. Suddenly, she grabbed the bucket beside her and started vomiting hard.

"Everlee, this time I want you to imagine the virus running through her as a color—we'll say it's a gross green. Picture in your mind light infiltrating it and it bursting into nothing and leaving her body."

Everlee nodded. "I'll try." She sat beside the still vomiting Lacey and placed one hand on her stomach and one on her back and pictured it just like Lional had told her. It took a while to get the image, but once she did, she slowly started breaking it up.

After a few minutes, Lacey didn't feel anymore sickness, and she lay back and relaxed; she was done puking. "Thanks, Evie, I feel much better. Just a little tired, but nothing a rest won't fix I think."

"You're welcome, Lace, I'm glad I could help."

"All right," Nurse Emily told her, "you lay there and rest a little bit, then I'll let you go." Lacey nodded, and they left.

Everlee's second and last charge for the day was a second-year boy. He had sprained his wrist, but Everlee healed it.

"Thanks," said the boy.

"You're welcome," she told him.

Everlee and the headmaster left for his office. Once in his office and seated, he began. "I'm impressed. You're doing very well. How do you feel after today's healings?"

"A bit more drained than usual but okay."

He nodded. "Well, I'll let you out early today. We have another half hour, but I want you to go take a small nap before lunch and warriors' training. I'll see you next week, and as always, my door is always open should you wish to come see me."

She nodded. "Thank you, sir." Everlee took off, and when she got to her room, she lay down and immediately passed out; she was so tired.

Suddenly, what felt like seconds later, she was being shaken awake by Sandy. "Come on, Evie, it's time for lunch. The headmaster saw me and told me to make sure you woke up for lunch."

"Thanks, Sandy," she said.

"No problem," Sandy replied. "Are you feeling okay? You look tired."

"Yeah, I'm okay," Evie said. "Just tired."

The girls made their way to the dining hall for lunch. Sandy was telling her about her morning, and Evie listened. She looked out one of the last windows before the dining hall and spotted Oreck relaxing by the water.

Chapter 14

A Saturday Afternoon and a Full Moon

After a delicious lunch of chili, cornbread, and a tall glass of milk. Everlee walked off to warriors practice hand in hand with Dametri.

"How are you feeling?" she asked him.

"I've been better," he said, "but after tonight, I'll start feeling better again."

"I was wondering, where do you guys go during the full moon? I know we can't go down there, but just curious, and are you all together or separated?"

He thought for a second, then said, "Well, if I tell you, just promise you'll never go there. I would hate for you to get hurt." She promised. "Well, it's on the first floor. The hallway to the right of the back door that ends at a black door, the one everyone thinks is a closet because it's not numbered." She nodded. "Well, it's not. There's a spiral staircase going down. We have a bathroom and a small dining area where dinner is waiting for us. We change into robes, and we get fed an hour early so we have time to eat before we go down another flight of stairs under the floor. We pull up the latch and yank up the board and descend. There are metal cages so we aren't too close together but can still chat, and there are screens between them.

"The headmaster locks us in. We don't mind being separated. We can still talk, and it's for our safety too, so if we lose our tempers, we don't hurt each other. Anyway, he returns in the morning. We go upstairs, change into our outfits, and leave."

"Thank you for telling me," Everlee said. He squeezed her hand. They made their way to practice.

"Welcome, my warriors," said Sergeant Hyde. "Well, you know the drill. Off you go now—run." And they ran the trails and then scaled the obstacle course. "That's enough for today. I know we have a full moon tonight. Next Saturday will be a bit longer than usual. Well done, you're dismissed."

Everlee and Dametri walked over to the flower field and found their friends hanging out.

"Hey, guys!" Rachel called while the rest waved at them.

"Hey," they chorused back, waving. They sat down, and Everlee watched as Cyrus sat on Sandy's shoulder. Sandy held her arm out toward Kyle, and Kiki jumped to her and then jumped back to Kyle and went up to his neck and nuzzled him. *Aww,* Evie thought. Jasper and Rowland's dog, Rocky, were chasing each other playfully, and Tucker was eating nuts on Lacey's lap with Sasha all happy. Evie looked down at Oreck. "You wanna play?" He shot up into the air and looked down at her, waiting. She laughed. "Okay, I'll take that as a yes." She stood up. "Hey, Dametri, can you hand me my water canteen?"

"Sure thing." He handed it to her.

She opened it, set it down at her feet, and looked at Oreck. "When I give the signal, breathe fire and evaporate them, okay?" She looked at the canteen, very much aware that her friends had stopped to watch. Out of the canteen rose the water. She raised her hands and cut through the water till there were four sections. She placed her hands around one section and brought her hands together to form a water ball. She moved her hands off, and with a quick movement, pointed her finger to the sky, sending it flying up to Oreck. She yelled out "Fyla!" and he shot it with fire. Everyone clapped. She did this three more times with him, and then he flew down low and hovered by her.

"Great job, Oreck. You're amazing. I love you," Everlee said while stroking Oreck's head, and then he went to go fly around.

"That was great!" Dametri and her friends cheered.

"Thanks," she said, "I love playing with him, and it's fun practice for us both."

A little while later, Headmaster Lional appeared. "Dametri, my dear boy, it's time."

Dametri nodded, hugged Evie, and kissed her cheek. "I'll see you tomorrow," he whispered.

"Wait, what about Sasha?" she asked him.

"Oh, she'll stay in my room. I'll take her there real quick."

"Okay." She nodded. "Bye." She waved at him as he took off.

Later on, the rest of them took off to get dinner—ham and mashed potatoes with green beans—and afterward, Evie decided to go to the library. "I'll see you guys later," she said to them. They waved.

Evie arrived at the library. There weren't too many students there at the moment. She went to the third floor, found a book on poetry, took it to the first floor, and sat down in one of the chairs by the fireplace. After a little while, she heard a loud cawing, followed by the librarian shushing, but it happened again, causing the librarian to go investigate. Evie had a feeling that she knew that call, so she went to go look too.

Just as she rounded the second floor, she heard the librarian scream. Midnight had cawed again, startling her. Evie saw her step back and fall over a stool.

"Sorry, ma'am," came Chad's voice, "Midnight didn't mean to be loud. He was just flirting."

"What?" the librarian asked. Chad showed her a book; it was a book on albino ravens, and there were pictures of them in it. "Well, tell him this is a library."

"Yes, ma'am," he said as he helped her up, and she hobbled away.

Everlee came over. "Hey, Chad."

"Hey," he said.

"How are you?" she asked him.

"I'm good. I was just picking up a book. I got to get going though, or I'm gonna be late for class. Take care, Everlee." He took off, and she waved after him.

Later on, Everlee went to her room and wrote to her parents. She then sent it off and collected her things to go take a bath. She went to the bathroom, ran a bath, got out, and headed off to her room for bed. Oreck was waiting for her, lying by the fireplace. Sandy wasn't back yet, but it wasn't curfew, so that was okay. It wasn't far off, maybe an hour, and Everlee was still tired. "Good night," she said to Oreck. He closed his eyes, and shortly after, so did she as she drifted off to sleep.

Chapter 15

An Attack

Suddenly, Everlee awoke. The castle was full of horns blowing and screams, and Oreck was standing over her, roaring in the direction of her door. She looked behind her. Sandy wasn't there, meaning she couldn't have been asleep long because Sandy wasn't back, meaning it wasn't curfew. Suddenly, her door shook, and she heard scratching on it and growling and howling. It started to shake as if it were being ran at. Then the door fell in, and inside stepped a werewolf. Its left foot was bleeding. Oreck spread out his wings and roared the loudest, fiercest roar at it, as if daring it to even try to come after Everlee. Unfortunately, it dared, and the minute it stepped forward, teeth bared toward Everlee, Oreck breathed fire at it, causing it to growl in pain and fall down. But it got back up, and this time, not missing a beat, Everlee stood next to Oreck and summoned a strong windstorm. She was surprised by the intensity of it but pleased, considering her opponent. Oreck breathed fire again, catching it in a swirling cyclone around the wolf, creating this fire tornado that paralyzed the wolf in fear.

Suddenly, she heard shouting. The night warriors and night sergeant was there, as was the headmaster. Valerie was a warrior, and she and the others, seeing as the wolf was distracted, blew a ton of sleeping darts at it. When about twenty hit the wolf, it collapsed in a heap, snoring.

Everlee and Oreck stopped, and the wind and fire disappeared, allowing the sergeant to come forward, muzzle the werewolf, and chain it up. Then the oldest, strongest boys helped carry it down to the holding area.

"We'll wait for you, Headmaster, by the door down there," called the sergeant. Headmaster Lional nodded. Valerie had run forward and was hugging Everlee.

"Are you okay?" asked Lional.

"Yes," Everlee said, "just, well, what the heck happened?"

"Somehow, one of the wolves got out of the holding area," said Valerie, "and it came tearing up to the girls' dorms, looking for you."

"Apparently, but why me?" Evie said.

"I don't know," said Valerie, "but thank God you're okay."

"Yes," said Lional. "I confess I was very concerned. Thank God you also had Oreck. By the looks of it, he was standing up very well to the wolf."

"Yes," said Everlee, "he was amazing."

"Headmaster, with your permission, can I stay here tonight to stand guard? Even if it's just to grant her some extra peace of mind. I'll leave before the sun rises."

"Yes, that sounds like a good idea. Everlee, come see me in the morning." She nodded. "I must go and get the werewolf back in its cage and do some investigating. Luckily, only one seemed to have gotten out. I'll be posting extra security at the door tonight and the rest on the grounds, myself included."

Suddenly, Sandy ran past the headmaster and into Evie's arms. "Oh, thank goodness you're okay!" she cried. "I was so scared when I heard it was headed to our room and saw the blood on the floor."

"I'm okay," Everlee said, stroking Sandy's hair. "It's okay."

"Good night, girls, please try to get some rest. You're safe, I promise. The holding area will be getting extra guards tonight, and if you hear some talking outside later, don't worry, I'll be having the teachers going around helping get everyone to bed, except for the vampire students." They nodded, and he left.

The girls sat on Everlee's bed, talking, and Everlee stroked Oreck's head and laid her head against his. "Thank you," she said to him. "I love you, Oreck." He made a contented, happy noise as she spoke to him.

"I like your room," Valerie said.

"Thanks," Sandy said.

"Well, you girls should get some sleep. It's okay, I'll keep watch."

"Thanks," said Sandy and Everlee. Everlee lay in bed with Oreck next to her. Sandy got in her nightdress, and the girls, with the exception of Valerie, went to sleep.

Sandy and Everlee awoke hours later. The sun was shining through her window. Valerie was gone, of course. Sandy and Everlee got dressed in the closet since they still didn't have a door.

"I hope the door is replaced soon," Sandy said.

"Me too," said Evie, and they headed to breakfast. As they were leaving, they saw the scorch marks, and it caused Everlee to shiver at the memory. They made it to the dining hall. Everyone seemed to be staring at Everlee. Rachel and Lacey, along with Grace and Hannah, ran up and hugged her.

"Are you girls okay?" they asked.

"Yes," said Everlee, "I'm okay."

"And I was with Kyle, so I'm okay too," said Sandy.

"Well, let's grab breakfast and then sit down and talk," said Rachel. "I want to hear all about it, and I have news for you on who attacked you."

"How do you know?" said Everlee.

"I went to the sick bay this morning, fearing you girls were hurt, but thank the Lord you're both okay, but I caught a glimpse of Gertrude lying in a bed with her left foot bandaged up. Nurse Emily wouldn't tell me anything though."

Everlee nodded. This was a lot of information to absorb. Why was Gertrude out last night, and why was she targeted? Surely this couldn't be over a boy, could it?

The girls got breakfast and sat down. Everlee just had a bowl of oatmeal; she wasn't that hungry. She told them everything from Oreck growling, standing over her, and protecting her to the door busting down, to the fire tornado, to how the warriors came and Valerie stayed with them, and to how the headmaster wanted her to see him that morning.

"Wow," they said.

"It's a good thing you were able to focus in that situation and fight back," said Hannah.

"It's a good thing she also had Oreck," said Lacey.

Evie nodded. "I'm so grateful to have Oreck," Everlee agreed.

"Where is he by the way?" Grace asked.

"He went outside. I think he is by the water. I'm gonna go out and hang out with him after I see the headmaster." They nodded. "Well, I'll see you girls later. I have to get going. I told the headmaster I'd see him this morning, and quite frankly, I want to know more information—if he has any and is willing to share it with me." With that, Everlee turned, took her tray, and dumped it, and then left the dining hall to go see the headmaster.

Just before she reached the headmaster's office, she heard her name being called. She turned; it was Dametri. He reached her and hugged her so tightly. After a few minutes, he let go and seemed to be scanning her up and down. "Thank God you're okay. I was so worried when I heard where Gertrude had gone off to."

"What happened last night in the holding cell?"

"Someone broke in. I couldn't see who. She wore a black cloak, but her face was hidden. I heard Gertie roar in pain, and the figure spoke something to her. I couldn't catch it all. I think it may have been a woman. Next thing I knew, there was a clank and a roar of pain. I think she stepped on a piece of mirror, and that's how she hurt her foot, and then the hooded figure left. I think the cloaked figure got spooked and heard something and then, not long after, was followed after by Gertrude."

Suddenly, Headmaster Lional appeared beside Everlee. "Thank you, Dametri, but I'll take it from here. You may hang out in a bit." Dametri nodded, whispered "I love you" to Everlee, and took off. Everlee turned around, followed the headmaster inside his office, closed the door behind her, and sat down in front of his desk as he sat down behind it.

Chapter 16

Learning More About Last Night

"So tell me, my dear, how are you doing, and please be truthful. I don't want to hear you're fine—how could you be fine after that?"

Everlee sat there and thought of how to answer that. "Well," she began, "I guess that's true. Last night's attack surprised me greatly, and I don't understand why I was targeted. Surely, it can't just be over a boy." He looked at her. "Gertie likes Dametri too," Evie said. "She isn't happy we started dating." He nodded. "Well, then there's the question of if it wasn't over a boy, then why me? Out of the whole school, why was I the only one she came after? How'd she have the focus to ignore everyone, and what about her foot? Dametri said it was a mirror she probably stepped on and that there was a cloaked figure—he thinks a female—but why let only her out, and how did she know where the holding area was, and how did she get in and get her out? Oh, and, sir, when can we have a new bedroom door so we're not feeling so exposed?"

"Well," he began, "you'll be happy then to hear that, at this moment, your bedroom door is being replaced and will be done today shortly."

She nodded. "That's good," she said, "thank you."

"As far as Gertrude, I don't know yet, my dear. I am investigating though. She was brought up to the sick bay this morning. She is cuffed by one arm to her bed. I don't enjoy treating a student like a prisoner, but for this case, it's for safety, at least till we get things figured out. I was going to go and question her. I was thinking you should come with me. It's okay to be scared, but just know she won't be able to hurt you. I'll be by your side the whole time."

"Okay," Everlee said, "I'll go with you. I want to know too."

"Okay," he said, "but first, please tell me what happened and how you and Oreck handled things before I arrived. I saw a fire tornado."

Evie nodded, and she told him everything, from Oreck standing guard over her to creating the fire tornado.

"I'm very impressed, and you two have a wonderful bond. It was good he was there." She nodded. "Well then," said Lional, "let us be off then, shall we?"

Everlee got up and followed Headmaster Lional out of his office. He closed and locked his door, and then they made their way to the sick bay. They walked into the sick bay. Gertrude seemed to be the only one in there this morning and was behind a screen. Nurse Emily came up to them.

"Oh, good Lord, Everlee, my dear, are you okay?"

Everlee nodded. "Physically, yes," she said. Nurse Emily nodded in an understanding way.

"How is Gertrude?" asked Lional.

"She's resting. I've bandaged up her foot. It had shards of the mirror she stepped on. I removed the fragments of mirror, and her hair was singed so much I had to cut it. It's now at her shoulder, and she has a bandaged upper forearm. It was burned—only a second degree though. She's lucky. From what I heard, she was in a fire tornado," she said, looking at Everlee at that last part. Evie nodded. "But there was something else," Nurse Emily said, looking back to Lional. "There was a slit on her back, on the left shoulder, and it had this gray substance with black spots in it crusted on her shoulder. I was gonna wipe it off but thought I'd wait for you since you said you were coming back soon. I don't know what it is, but I am hoping you will."

Lional nodded. "Very well, let me see her. Come along, Everlee, dear." They followed Nurse Emily behind the screen, where Gertie was sleeping. She looked a bit banged up with her foot and arm all bandaged and her hair cut to her shoulders now, but it still looked cute on her, so maybe she wouldn't be too upset about her hair.

Headmaster Lional bent down and pushed her nightgown's short sleeve up and over. He looked at her shoulder, put his finger in the substance, and sniffed it. After a minute, he turned, took a washcloth, dipped it in the bowl of water by Gertrude's bed, cleaned her shoulder off, and examined the wound. "There, that's better. We want this off her," he said. "It appears to be a hallucinogen and a hypnotic mixture. I bet that whoever realized her used this to put her in a trance with a specific goal. It would explain why Everlee was only targeted and not more students, but let's wake her and talk to her. Nurse Emily, may we have some time alone, please?" She nodded and left them.

Lional gently shook Gertie awake. She looked up at him and Everlee. "What's going on?" she asked him. "Why is she here, and why am I injured?" She reached up, touched her hair, and squeached. "And what happened to my hair!"

"Calm down, dear girl, your hair is the least of your worries." She quieted down, but the look on her face said that her hair was a big concern. "What do you remember from last night after you went to the holding area?"

She appeared deep in thought. "It's in pieces, and I don't understand some of them."

"Tell me what you remember, and we'll help you piece them together so we can all understand better."

She nodded. "Well, I was sitting in my cage in pain from the transformation process starting. I was still dwelling over Dametri telling me off. We grew up together, and he's siding with her," she said, nodding toward Everlee.

Evie didn't know they had known each other their whole lives, but she'd never asked. He had told her they were friends. She never thought to ask for how long.

"And then," said Gertrude, continuing, "I felt a pain in my shoulder and fell to the floor. Suddenly, my rage worsened. I saw the bottom of a black cloak but didn't see who it was. I remember it was a girl's voice, but no one I remember. She whispered something, but I don't remember it much—something about 'find and destroy her.' I was already angry at Everlee before I transformed, mind you. I may despise her, but I'm not a killer, unless it's an animal during a hunt back home.

"I started feeling fuzzy in my head and kept hearing her say "Everlee," and I couldn't get the thought out of my head. It was like it was locked in, and then she left, and I fell to the ground for a minute. My rage built up higher till I started hitting the cage, but somehow, it had been unlocked 'cause it swung open. I stepped on something sharp 'cause I felt pain hit my foot, then I remember screams, and my brain felt fuzzy, like I was there, but yet I wasn't. It felt like my body wasn't under my control. Next thing I knew, I'm staring at a door, then I was surrounded by fire and more yelling. I felt things hit me, and I blacked out. That's all I remember, I swear. Everlee," Gertie said to her, "I'm so sorry. Yes, it's no secret I don't like you, but I swear, I would never have tried to kill you. Tease and torment, sure, but I'm not a killer."

Everlee nodded. While she didn't like Gertrude, she felt the sincerity in her voice. "I believe you," Everlee told her.

"So what happened to my hair?" Gertie said.

"That was me," Everlee said. "The fire from Oreck and the fire tornado, but it was in self-defense."

She groaned. "Great," she said, "just great. Well, I guess it'll grow back. Does Dametri hate me? Surely he can't think I knew what I was doing at the time? Like I said, my body felt like it wasn't under my control, like I was a puppet, if that makes sense."

Headmaster Lional finally spoke, "I believe you, Gertrude. The wound on your shoulder was laced with drugs and would have made you open to suggestion, however, I want you to stay here for a few days. Get stronger, okay?"

She nodded. "Thank you, sir, for believing me."

"In the meantime," he continued, "please try to get along with each other, and I will be sending out a search party to see if we can find a trace of this intruder. I'll have the grounds staffed with warriors—taking shifts, of course—for sleeping and class purposes, so everyone isn't stuck on guard duty and still has time for class and free time while also taking turns helping and protecting us during the week, night and day. On the next full moon, I, too, will stand guard outside the holding area. Rest assured, the intruder must be mad if she thinks we won't be on alert after this. You come to me, Gertrude, if people harass you for this. While I don't condone your going after Everlee verbally, I will not have you attacked for something you couldn't control last night."

She nodded. "Thank you, sir."

"And, Everlee, I'll also have your room under guard on the next full moon—one person outside and one inside at night."

She nodded. "Thank you, Headmaster."

"Well, let us go so Ms. Gertrude can get some rest. Everlee, if you're willing and Gertrude is willing, I'll have you come up later tonight to heal Ms. Gertrude."

Evie nodded, and they took off. "So, sir, may I ask, will I be informed when you know more, or is it none of my concern?"

"No, you're fine. I will send for you when and if I learn more." She nodded. "And between us, I'll also be looking at the holding area and into the possibility of it being someone from the inside."

"Do you think someone in here did this?"

"It's a possibility, but just stay sharp." She nodded. "Well, my dear," Headmaster Lional said, stopping and looking out the window, "by the looks of things, your friends and Oreck are by the waterfall, why don't you go see them and try to enjoy your afternoon. Oh, and, Everlee?"

"Yes, sir?" she said, looking at him.

"Happy Halloween."

"Happy Halloween." She smiled before taking off to go outside and enjoy the day and, of course, to tell Dametri about Gertrude.

Yes, they didn't like each other, but she believed Gertie didn't have control, and so being the bigger person, she wanted to tell Dametri so he wouldn't go hating her. At least this time, if Gertrude decided to go all mean in the future, then Everlee was not responsible for that friendship going extinct. Time would tell; for now, she was going relax and wish her friends and boyfriend a happy Halloween and have some caramel apple later, apparently, because she smelled the caramel coming from the direction of the kitchen.

Chapter 17

A Plan

It was a week away to the next full moon. Everything was almost back to normal, with the exception of the ongoing investigation from last month's attack. So far, the headmaster had discovered that the mirror was a witch's glass, meaning that it may not have been a female under the cloak; it may have been a female voice coming from the mirror, but it also could have been a female. They would find out, he assured her. But otherwise, Everlee and Dametri were as happy together as ever. Gertrude was out from the hospital and, so far, had been ignoring her. She was being civil, talking to her only while Dametri was around, just stuff like hello and goodbye, but mainly just talking to Dametri. And Oreck was now living in a cave next to the waterfall that Everlee, with permission, had made for him. Thank goodness for her gifts. It was a big cave, and he loved it in there, and when he wasn't in the cave, he was flying in the sky, usually accompanied by Cyrus. He would even poke his head up to the windows to check on Everlee or say hey in his own way. Everybody thought he was awesome, although sometimes, he startled the teachers when doing that. Everlee always visited him every day, and especially before bed, she would visit him at his cave. Oreck was so closely bonded to her he would usually swing by her window afterward for a second good night hug from Everlee.

Oreck was now the size of a fully grown horse, not counting his tail and his wingspan. He was truly magnificent to behold. She missed having him in her room but still felt safe knowing he was nearby. He wouldn't let anyone hurt her, and if she was to call for him, she knew without a doubt that even if he were sleeping, he'd awaken and be over to her as fast as possible.

Everlee was done with classes for the day and was watching Oreck fly up in the sky. Cyrus was flying with him; they were buddies. She was next to the waterfall and would occasionally shoot a water ball up to him and yell "Fyla!" and he'd attack it with fire.

Suddenly, Sandy, Rachel, and Lacey showed up.

"Hey," Everlee said to them. They smiled, chorused "Hey" back, and sat down by her.

"So where's Dametri?" Rachel asked her.

"Oh, he's off at the library. I'll see him at dinner. I just wanted to hang outside with Oreck. Speaking of boyfriends, where's Kyle?" she asked Sandy.

"He said he was gonna go hang with Dametri, so I guess the library." Evie nodded, and the girls sat and talked. Before long, Everlee bid Oreck goodbye for a little bit to go eat dinner. After dinner, Everlee and Dametri visited Oreck in his cave.

"Where's Sasha?" she asked him.

"Oh, she's off in my room napping." He laughed.

Everlee told Oreck good night, hugged him, and walked back to her room. Shortly after, Dametri kissed her good night at her door and then left. She went inside, changed into pajamas, and wrote her parents a letter. They still wanted to send out extra security but had held off so far. She sent the letter off, and she was sitting in her chair by the fireplace and reading the book on regeneration when she heard Oreck gently roar to her outside her window. She grinned, went over to the window, pulled back the curtains. There he was.

"Good night," she told him while he poked his head in slightly, and she hugged and stroked him. "I love you." He closed his eyes happily and took off moments later. She laughed. He was so sweet, but yet anyone would have to be insane to try and take him on. He was very protective of Everlee, and she absolutely loved him.

Suddenly, Sandy came in.

"Hey," said Everlee, sitting back in her chair beside the fireplace, lighting a fire with her gift.

"Ooh, I do enjoy a good fire," said Sandy, coming over and sitting down a few minutes after changing into her pajamas.

"Me too. So how was your evening with Kyle?" she asked Sandy.

Sandy smiled and said, "Oh, it was magical. We sat out in the field on a blanket, looking up at the stars and moon, and he sang me a song his mother used to sing to him while growing up. It was beautiful. He has a lovely voice. Then we slow danced a little under the stars and kissed, before he walked me to my room, and we said good night." She was definitely in love; Evie could see it on her face and hear it in her voice. Everlee was happy for her.

"So do you think, one day, after we graduate, you would move to the elfin village with him?"

"Yes, I think I would. He tells me it's beautiful there, but nothing can compare to my beauty."

"Aww," said Everlee, "you two are adorable together."

"Thanks," Sandy said. "So what are you up to?"

"Oh, I sent off a letter to Mom and Dad. They still wanted to send security, but I told them it's okay, so we'll see, and Oreck was just by the window a few minutes ago for a second good night." She laughed. "Speaking of which, where's Cyrus?" she asked Sandy.

"Oh, he is outside. He'll be back soon." And right on cue, Cyrus flew in the window and landed on Sandy's shoulder. "Hello," Sandy cooed at him while nuzzling her head against him. He closed his eyes and seemed happy. "So how's the book?" Sandy asked, looking at the regeneration book Evie was holding.

"It's good," she said.

"Is there anything on the person that had the gift before you in there?" asked Sandy.

"Only a little bit so far. From what I've read, I know it was a female. She was an elf. Her name was Maureen, and her dragon was black and red. She called him Abraxas."

"So what happened to her?" Sandy asked. "If she was an elf, shouldn't she still be around?"

"I'm not sure. Maybe it's further in the book, but if and when I find out, I'll let you know."

Sandy seemed pleased that Everlee was going to tell her. "Well, we should get to bed," she said.

"Yes," agreed Evie, and they got in bed and turned off the lamps. "Should I turn the fireplace off?" Evie asked her.

"No, let's leave it on tonight."

"Okay," Evie said and rolled over and drifted off to sleep.

A few days had passed when Everlee was told by Ms. Perdy that the headmaster wished to see her, so she took off to his office. She knocked. "Come in," he called. She did and closed the door behind her before proceeding to sit in the chair before his desk.

"You wanted to see me, sir?"

"Yes, I did," he said. "I'm about to go and talk with the werewolf students in the dining hall. Tonight is the full moon, so their senses are heightened. I'm thinking they can smell out the person from the holding area, and we can catch them."

"So you definitely think it's a person on the inside?" Everlee asked.

"I do, but I don't think they are the main culprit. The mirror suggests there are others, but I'm determined to find out who is responsible for last month, and we don't have much time, so please, I just wanted to let you know. Now when you go back to class, don't tell anybody about this." She nodded. "Stay here, please, I'll be right back." And he took his orb out and went into the fireplace, and minutes later, out came twenty-five soldiers and Lieutenant Green, followed by the headmaster. Then he turned off the fireplace.

Everlee was in shock. "Sir," she began, "what is this? Why the soldiers?"

He gave her a sympathetic smile. "My dear girl," began Lional, "I know you didn't think the soldiers were needed, but your parents and I do. Please trust me on this. If the culprit is in the school, I don't want them getting away, so the extra security, the better." She nodded. "All right then, off you go."

"Thank you, sir," she said, taking off and back to Ms. Perdy's class, and waited for the search to begin sometime that day.

Chapter 18

Sniffing Out the Culprit

Later on, Everlee was outside by the waterfall with her peers for meditation.

"Where are the werewolf students?" Hannah whispered to Grace. "I haven't seen them since second period was over."

"I heard they went down to the dining hall. I wonder what for," Hannah said.

"Ladies, pay attention, please!" called Ms. Bell. They blushed but quieted down.

"Hey, Everlee," Jack whispered to her while they stretched, "what's up with the soldiers?" She looked. "I saw them come out of the headmaster's office earlier before mediation started." She shrugged, and he gave her a look as if he didn't believe her. "So tell me," he whispered again when Ms. Bell's head was turned away, "are you worried? Tonight's the full moon." She gave him a shredded look. "Hey, don't get mad, I just mean, with last month's attack, are you scared for tonight?"

"Why are you so worried?" she asked.

"Just asking," he said.

"No," she said, "I know that I will be fine." He shut up after that. Suddenly, the headmaster and two wolf students, Gertrude and Dametri, showed up, along with Lieutenant Green and a soldier.

"May I interrupt, please," he said to Ms. Bell.

"Of course," she said.

"Now, class, as we speak, there are wolf students accompanying soldiers and searching the school for the possibility of someone here that may have let Ms. Gertrude out last month, and we are here to check out your class. This won't take long, and then if no one is found, we'll leave.

"Line up now, please, a straight line in front of me. Now if they find someone, they will ring the bell to alert me, as will I, if I find it's one of you. As I'm sure you know, werewolves have excellent noses, especially during a full moon. We don't have long though before they must go into holding, so let's make this simple. Dametri and Gertrude will walk by and smell you, and if they recognize the culprit's scent, they will be taken into custody immediately." Everyone nodded.

"Surely, sir, they can't possibly remember what the person smelled like from last month," said Jack.

"Oh yes, I can," said Gertrude and Dametri together so fast.

Headmaster Lional spoke up, "Yes, my dear boy, they can."

"And I can smell the person right now," said Gertrude as she walked past them. Gertie was in front of the group and Dametri in the back.

"So can I," Dametri said. They cornered Jack.

"It's him!" yelled Gertie, full of anger. Dametri grabbed Jack's shirt.

"That's enough," said Lional. "Lieutenant, please take him and follow me. Classes are over for the day, and, Evie, I'll send for you later," he called back to her as he walked off. She nodded.

Jack tried to run but was tackled and dragged off, yelling, "This is ridiculous!" Suddenly, his eagle came swooping down, screeching and biting at the soldiers. Arden went head-to-head with him, and Sergeant Hyde ran out from the academy, threw a net over Jack's eagle, caught it, and carried it inside behind them. Lional whispered to the other warrior, who had followed behind the sergeant. Then minutes later, the bell chimed, signaling the search was over. Everlee and everyone else were in shock.

"Oh my gosh!" Grace exclaimed.

Dametri hugged Evie. "It's okay," he said.

"Thank you," she said to him and turned her head to Gertie. "And thank you," she said to her. Gertie nodded to her.

Robert and Aiden were talking, and Everlee caught bits and pieces. "What in the world was he thinking?" and something about "I thought he was a bit of a jerk, but I never thought he'd do this." They shook their heads.

Hannah was crying. "Are you okay?" Grace asked her.

"Yes, I just can't believe someone in here tried to have Everlee killed."

"Hey, I'm okay," Evie said, patting Hannah's back. She nodded and calmed down. "What's gonna happen to his familiar, Arny?" Evie asked Dametri.

But Gertrude spoke up first. "There are three options—they will put the animal down, he'll have to go live alone, or he'll go to the familiar sanctuary for those that have lost a bonded companion. It will be up to the headmaster. It was in a book I read in the library last year." Evie nodded.

"All right, class, why don't you all go inside till dinner?" called Ms. Bell. They nodded and went inside.

"Come to my window in a little bit," Everlee called to Oreck.

Dametri and Kyle, who had joined them inside, walked Evie and Sandy to their bedroom. "Are you sure you don't want to hang out?" Kyle asked Sandy.

"Not right now, I'm sorry. I think Evie and I are gonna write our parents and take a small nap if we can quiet our minds, but come back and walk us to dinner later," she said to him. He nodded.

"And I'll come back before dinner so I can say good night to you before I go into the holding area for the night." Evie nodded at Dametri. The boys bid the girls farewell till later.

Inside, they sat down and wrote letters to their parents. Everlee made sure to ask how long the soldiers would be staying and then sent the letters off. Oreck popped by their window just then. Everlee stroked his head. "Hey, boy, what a day, huh?" He gently grumbled in agreement. "Well, I'll see you after dinner, okay? You go have fun, but stay safe, all right?" He gave a little roar and took off.

"Let's get some rest," Evie said.

"Yes," agreed Sandy.

"This is a lot to process. I have a feeling it's just the beginning," said Everlee, and they lay down and went to bed.

Later, there was knocking on their door. They sat up and stretched. Rubbing her eyes, Everlee walked over, opened the door, and saw Lieutenant Green. "The headmaster would like to see you, Princess."

Everlee nodded. "I'll see you later," she said to Sandy and took off. On the way to the headmaster, she passed Dametri.

"Evie, what's going on? I was just coming to see you before I went to the holding area. Are you okay?"

Evie walked to the side and pulled Dametri with her. "The headmaster wants to see me."

"I'll walk you." Lieutenant Green started to say "It wasn't necessary," when Everlee cut in. "I insist." And he quieted.

They reached the office of Headmaster Lional. She hugged Dametri. "I love you, and I'll see you in the morning," she said, giving him a kiss.

"I love you too," he said, and then he took off.

Inside was the headmaster; Lieutenant Green stayed outside. "Where are the soldiers and Jack? What's gonna happen to his familiar, Arny?"

"Please take a seat, my dear," Lionel said, gesturing to the chairs in front of his desk. She did as he asked. "The soldiers," he began, "are throughout the school and grounds. Jack has been taken by me and two soldiers to the prison area where the rogue wolves are also being held. He is refusing to talk, other than to insist that Arny should be shown mercy. He insisted that his familiar didn't have a hand in this, and I believe that part, so Arny will be sent to the familiar sanctuary so he won't be alone. There are other familiars there and a few humans that have lost their familiars, and they all take care of each other. It's a lovely place. He'll miss Jack and be sad, but it's his best option."

Evie nodded. "But, sir, how are we gonna get Jack to talk to us and tell us what happened?"

"Time, my dear. Until he does, we know where to find him. I have to get ready to put the wolf students into the holding area, and at dinner, I'll make a speech. How are you taking things though, my dear?" he asked her.

She replied, "Honestly, sir, I'm shocked. I can't believe this. Although today in meditation, Jack was acting weird, so I guess now I know why."

He nodded. "Rest assured, my dear girl, you're safe, and I'm always here. The soldiers will be staying tonight and heading back tomorrow, provided nothing happens." She nodded. "Now, my dear, if you hurry, you can find Dametri for one last good night before he goes away for the night."

She smiled. "Thank you, sir," she said, and took off to find Dametri, tell him what she learned, and kiss him really quick. Luckily, she found him about to go down the stairs to the first floor and told him. He nodded, and they kissed a great kiss. Just then, he heard other wolf students heading their way.

"I'll see you in the morning." He smiled at her, kissed her again, and took off. She stared as he left, then took off to her room to walk to dinner with Sandy and Kyle in a little bit.

Chapter 19

A Favor and Dresses

It was now December. Jack was still locked up. The other day, Everlee had visited the headmaster's office to see if there was any new information. "I'm afraid he's still keeping it private. I do think the main person behind everything is a female though. For one, there was a female voice no one recognized, which led me to believe it came from the mirror. Secondly, when questioned about the mirror and the female voice, he looked nervous but stayed quiet. I just have this feeling, and most of the time, my feelings are right."

"And the wolves in the prison, sir?" she asked.

He sighed. "Just like Jack, they still won't budge. I think some are scared of this person and some are just outright loyal and some are being used but won't say what the person has on them or whom."

She nodded. "Thank you, sir, I hope we find a break soon."

He nodded. "Me too, my dear."

"Well, I'll be going now," she said.

"All right, my dear, thank you for the visit." She nodded and left.

The rest of Everlee's classes went smoothly. It was now a week away from the dance, and the girls were starting to get excited. It became the main topic you hear no matter where you went. Everlee couldn't blame them though. The dresses and tux or dress apparel for the guys were all due to arrive tomorrow, six days before the dance. Even she looked forward to seeing her dress.

It was evening, and Everlee was out in the cave with Oreck. She had made a fire, and they were enjoying it. She talked to Oreck about what she had found out, and he seemed to listen intently. "Any ideas on who this female could be?" she asked him. He shook his head and sneezed. She laughed. "Yeah, me neither, but I intend to find out," she told him.

Suddenly, there was a knock on the outside of the cave. "May I come in?" a voice called. She recognized that voice; it was Chad. "Yes, come on in," she called. Soon after, Chad came in with Midnight on his shoulder and sat down by the fire.

"Nice," he said, looking at the fire and around the cave.

"Thanks," she replied.

"You made this yourself?" he asked. She nodded. He looked impressed. "So how are you?" he asked her.

"I'm all right, you?" she asked him.

He thought for a minute. "Well," he began, "a mixture. I am glad you're still here and angry at Jack, but I am also nervous."

"Why are you nervous?" she asked him.

"Because of the dance. I really like Hannah a lot, and I was thinking if things go well at the dance, I would see if she wanted to be my girlfriend."

"Aww—" Everlee started.

But Chad spoke up. "No, Evie, not 'aww.' I can't dance. What if I am bad at it?"

She stood up. "Well, I'll help you," she said.

"You will?" he replied. "But how?"

"I'll teach you how to slow dance, and I'll have Dametri teach you tomorrow how to do some basic dance moves. We can practice in here so no one knows."

"Thanks, Evie. He won't tell, right?"

She shook her head. "No, he's a good guy." Chad looked relieved. "Now place your hands on my waist," she said after putting her hands on his shoulders. He did but looked nervous. "Now just move, kinda sway a little as you move in a slow circle. It's okay, you're doing good."

He smiled. "Thanks, Evie. So why are you helping me?" he asked as they danced.

"Because I think you and Hannah would be cute together, and you're a nice guy." Suddenly, Midnight cawed. "You're a good bird too," Everlee said to Midnight, causing him to caw again in happiness. They laughed and stopped dancing.

"So," Everlee said, sitting down, "anymore incidents in the library?"

Chad laughed. "Yeah, I don't think the librarian likes us, but he just gets excited." She laughed and nodded. Suddenly, the bell chimed. "Well, I better go get to class," he said.

"Same, I gotta get to my room and head to bed." She hugged Oreck and told him good night. "I'll see you in a few at the window," she whispered, and they took off. Chad walked her to the second floor. "Bye." She waved at him.

She got to her room, changed, and said a second good night to Oreck. Sandy came in, and the girls talked for a few minutes before heading to bed.

The next day went by with lots of excited giggling. Their dresses were coming today. Everlee pulled Dametri to the side after lunch and asked him to teach Chad how to dance later and how she taught him to slow dance last night. "Don't worry though, he's just a friend. He's hoping to ask Hannah to be his girlfriend if things go well at the dance, so will you help?" she asked.

"Of course."

"Wonderful," she said. "It's tonight after dinner in the cave, okay? And please keep it a secret."

He nodded. "I will," he said. Everlee smiled and kissed him before heading off to class.

Girls and guys were called out all day to pick up their garments and take them to their rooms before returning to class. Sandy and Everlee got called down a few minutes before their last class ended. Sandy and Everlee took their bags to their rooms and opened them. Since it was so late, they didn't have to go back to class.

Sandy's dress was gorgeous. She squealed in delight. "Oh, I love it!" she exclaimed.

"It's gorgeous," Evie told her. Sandy's dress was a royal purple with a sweetheart neckline and silver cap sleeves. It had a silver line running down the middle, and she had silver flats for her shoes. Her dress went all the way to her ankles, and she had silver and purple bangles for her wrists.

"Your turn, let's see yours," Sandy said.

"Okay." Evie grinned and took her dress out. The dress had spaghetti straps with a sweetheart neckline. It was long, going to her ankles. A black-and-blue ombré, it started out black, then when about a foot away from the bottom of the dress, it turned to this beautiful deep royal blue. The dress puffed out slightly around the waist area on down. She didn't want heels, so she had black flats. Everlee also had a small silver tiara with blue gems.

"That's beautiful, Evie!" Sandy exclaimed.

"Thank you," she smiled. She was thrilled at how it turned out.

There was a knock on the door. She opened it, and there stood Rachel and Lacey with their dress bags.

"Can we come in?" Rachel asked.

"Of course," Evie said.

Just before she closed the door, Hannah and Grace showed up. "Can we come in too?" they chorused.

Everlee laughed. "All right." After they came inside, she closed the door.

The girls loved Sandy's and Evie's dresses. "Show us yours," Sandy said. Evie and Sandy put their dresses away in the closet and then sat and watched as the girls showed off their dresses.

Rachel's dress was a deep red form-fitting and strapless gown that went down to her ankles. She had red high heels and a gold necklace with a green emerald on it. "Beautiful!" they all told her. She blushed.

Next was Grace's. She had a short knee-length dress. It was dark pink, A-line, and sleeveless, together with black heels and black bangles for her wrists. "That's gonna look perfect on you," they all told her.

Next was Hannah's. Her dress was floor-length to her ankles. It had a high neck with spaghetti straps. The dress was a sparkly silver, and she had on sparkly silver high-heeled shoes, a black choker necklace with a red rose charm in the middle of it, and one single black bangle for her wrist. "Wow!" everyone exclaimed. "That's so pretty!"

"And shiny," Grace practically shouted, causing everyone to laugh.

"Thanks," said Hannah, "I like sparkly things." She giggled.

And last but not least was Lacey. Her dress was a floor-length one with a sweetheart neckline and off-shoulder cap sleeves. It was golden, and the top half was a sparkly gold and the bottom from the waist down was a pretty plain gold; it puffed out a bit from the waist down. She had sparkly golden flats for shoes and a black velvet choker necklace with two golden hearts intertwined in the middle.

"Wow!" everyone exclaimed.

"You're gonna look amazing," Rachel told her, and everyone nodded.

"Thanks," Lacey replied.

"Wait till the guys see us in these," Rachel said.

"They're gonna be speechless!" said Grace. Everyone laughed.

Chapter 20

The Dance

It was the night of the dance, and then tomorrow they would be going home for two weeks before returning to the academy. Some students, who had chosen to, would be staying at the academy over break. The headmaster was going to send Sandy, Cyrus, Oreck, and Everlee all home together. They were to meet at Oreck's cave tomorrow after breakfast. After they were sent home, the headmaster was going to send everyone else that needed help home.

"Are you already packed?" Sandy said, coming in the room and heading to the closet. "I still haven't even started," Sandy continued. "Why did I put it off till today!" she groaned.

Evie grinned. "Sandy, it's okay. We don't have to pack."

Sandy stopped and turned to Everlee. "Why not?" she asked.

"Because I have plenty more clothes at home, as you know, and I was thinking you could stay in my room. I'll even let you use my clothes. It'll be fun. What do you think?"

Sandy squealed in delight. "That would be wonderful! Oh, thanks, Evie!" She grinned.

Evie laughed. "No problem. So since we're not packing, I'm gonna go down and see Oreck. Wanna come?" she asked.

"Yeah, that sounds good," Sandy said as they left the room and locked up behind them.

They were sitting in the cave a few minutes later. Oreck had been flying with Cyrus, but they came down and followed them into his cave. "Hey," Everlee said while stroking the side of Oreck's head. "Tonight's the dance, okay? And then when I get back to my room, I'll call for you to say good night, okay?" He touched his head to hers. "And tomorrow, we go home for two weeks, and you'll meet my mom and dad. They are gonna fall in love with you, just like I did, so don't be scared, okay?"

Everlee sat down next to Oreck, and Cyrus was on Sandy's shoulders as the girls talked for a bit. Sandy had been in the cave before many times but was always amazed that Everlee built it. "You really are talented, Evie," she said in awe.

"Thanks, Sandy, but so are you, and I mean that." Sandy smiled. "We should go get lunch," Evie said. "I'll see you tonight, and maybe I'll call for you before the dance so you can see my dress, okay?" Evie told Oreck. He roared gently. The girls left, but Cyrus decided to stay back with Oreck.

"I love how good friends they are," Sandy said.

Evie nodded in agreement. "Me too," she said. They grabbed lunch—tall glasses of milk for both of them, and they both got pork chop, mashed potatoes, and green beans. Lunch was a bit more like dinner today, and at the dance, they would have sandwiches and cookies. They were told to eat as they got hungry and also that they could eat as much as they wanted. The dance was to be held in the dining hall. There were even rumors that a band was coming to play for the dance.

The girls found Kyle and Dametri and joined them. Soon after, Rachel and Lacey joined them. "Hey," Rachel said to everyone at the table. They all conversed and, soon after, departed, but not before Sandy and Everlee gave their boyfriends a kiss.

"Kyle and I will come to your rooms later to take you to the dance." The girls nodded, and a few minutes later, they were back in their bedroom.

Sandy and Everlee were about to go across the hall and get washed up when there was a knock on the door. Everlee opened it, and standing there was Lieutenant Green. "My princess," he began, "I know you're curious why I have come. Your parents have sent me and some other soldiers to have as extra security tonight since the warriors would be at the dance."

Everlee nodded. "Thank you," she told him, to which he nodded and took off.

Sandy and Everlee went and got washed up. They came back in their robes and put their dirty clothes in the hamper. Evie started a fire for them to cozy up to and also help their hair dry faster.

Later that evening, after Evie and Sandy had put on their dresses, there was a knock on the door. Sandy opened it with Evie right beside her. Standing on the other side was Kyle and Dametri.

"You look lovely, sweetheart," said Kyle to Sandy as she walked out to him.

"And you," said Dametri, reaching down to hold her hand after Evie locked their room, "look stunning."

She blushed. "Thank you," she told him.

They made their way to the dining hall, and when they stepped inside, they were amazed. It was snowing from the ceiling, but it evaporated before it hit the floor so the floors stayed dry, and it wasn't cold because there were a dozen little firepits set up around the room and fireflies flying around like stars. The room was dimmed, and there was a table on the left with punch and cookies and sandwiches. There were a few tables on the right side, and the middle was cleared so people could dance. The headmaster and teachers' table had been cleared, and a band was playing. They were called the Musical Hearts and were really good.

"Would you like a drink?" Dametri asked Evie. She nodded. "Okay, I'll be right back," he said and took off. Kyle left to grab Sandy a drink as well.

"Ugh," said Sandy suddenly.

"What is it?" asked Evie.

"Over by Dametri, look, it's Gertie."

Everlee looked, and sure enough, there Gertie was in a tight, form-fitting, one-shouldered, emerald-green velvet dress that stopped just above her knees. Evie just shook her head and turned away.

"Oh look, there's Valerie." Valerie was dancing with her date. She looked stellar in her dress. It was a form-fitting strapless black mermaid dress with a straight neckline. It also had a dark-red stripe along the sides.

"She looks great," Sandy said. Evie nodded, and they waved at her. She waved back. The girls spotted Hannah and Chad dancing and laughing; Midnight was up in the snow, cawing and trying to catch the snow in his beak. People thought it was funny. Grace, Rachel, and Lacey were all dancing with their dates too.

Suddenly, Kyle came back with Dametri. "Sorry about the wait. Kyle was waiting for me, but Gertie came up and started chatting. I broke away as soon as I could."

Evie smiled and kissed him. "It's okay. Thank you for my drink," she said, taking it. They finished their drinks and joined their friends on the dance floor. The headmaster and teachers were there too. After all, this was a school. Gertie looked a bit sore but didn't bother them. After a few minutes, she rejoined her date, who looked amazed to be with her. They danced the night away, taking a break here and there to sit and eat.

Finally, it was over. The boys walked Sandy and Everlee to their room and bid them good night.

"I'll see you in two weeks," Everlee said, kissing Dametri.

"And I am already counting till I'm back with you. I love you."

"I love you too," Everlee said back.

The girls were back in their room a few minutes later. Everlee and Sandy changed into their pajamas. Cyrus was on the chair by the fireplace. Evie walked to the window, pulled back the curtain, and called out for Oreck, and moments later, he appeared.

"Good night, Oreck. I love you, and I'll see you tomorrow, okay?" She hugged him as best as she could before he took off. "Well, we should get to bed," she said to Sandy, who nodded. They crawled into their beds after turning off all but the fireplace and one light. Tomorrow, Everlee would go home and see her parents. Tonight had been wonderful. They drifted off to sleep within minutes.

Chapter 21

Another Attack

The next morning at breakfast, Everlee and her boyfriend and friends all sat together. "I'm gonna miss you guys," Rachel said to them at the table.

"We'll miss you too," Everlee said. Everyone nodded and chorused in agreement.

A few minutes later, after breakfast had finished and Sandy and Everlee had said their goodbyes, the girls headed outside to Oreck's cave. Once they got to his cave, Cyrus flew down onto Sandy's shoulder and nuzzled up to her. Oreck came down from the sky and landed next to his cave. Moments later, the headmaster arrived.

"All ready to go?" They nodded. "Very well then, step back, please." He took out his orb, whispered to it, and rolled it gently into the cave, and the gold flames appeared. "Don't worry, it won't hurt you," he said. They nodded. "You'll come out in your garden. I modified the spell to project you somewhere besides a fireplace." He smirked. "Both your parents will be waiting for you, and I'll come and collect you in two weeks, okay?"

"Yes, sir," they chorused.

"Goodbye, girls."

They waved and stepped into the flames. "Come on, Oreck," Evie called over her shoulder, and he followed. What felt like seconds later, they emerged at the garden back home, and Everlee's mom and dad and

Sandy's mother came over to them, hugging them tightly and looking at Cyrus and Oreck—especially Oreck—in awe.

"So who's your familiar, darling?" Sandy's mother asked her.

"This is Cyrus." He hooted in greeting.

"Hi," they greeted him.

"And this must be Oreck," Everlee's father said.

"Yes," Everlee spoke up, "this is Oreck."

"Magnificent!" he muttered.

"Dad, where is he gonna stay? I haven't built him a cave yet."

"No worries, my dear, I built a fine cave for him over here." They followed him, and sure enough, he had built a fine cave. Oreck roared happily and walked inside to check it out and then came back and lay in the front.

"He likes it." Everlee laughed.

"Well, I'm glad," her father said. "Well, let's go inside. You can come out again later, and we can get to know Oreck more. I'm sure he'd like to rest in his new cave a bit."

Everlee nodded and hugged Oreck. "I love you, and I'll be out later, okay?" Cyrus flew over and landed by Oreck. "See, Cyrus will play and keep you company till we come out, okay?" They went inside.

"He's wonderful, sweetie," her mom said.

"Thanks, Mom," Everlee said.

"Where are your bags, girls?" Sandy's mom asked.

"I didn't pack one." Her mom looked at Everlee.

"It's my fault. I told her not to. I thought we could share a room, maybe, and I have plenty of clothes she can wear."

"Can I room with her?" Sandy's mom nodded, and Everlee's parents agreed too.

The next two weeks flew by. Everyone loved Oreck and thought Cyrus was cute. Sandy and Everlee showed their parents what they could do, and Everlee showed them her and Oreck's game. They were all impressed.

"I can't believe tomorrow after breakfast we go back already."

"I know, I'm gonna miss them."

"Me too," Sandy said, "but it will be nice to see everyone else again." Evie nodded.

Suddenly, she felt off and saw an undead man lunging toward her. Everlee ran; it had to be Oreck. She felt dread and anger.

"What's wrong?" Sandy yelled after her, but Everlee just kept running.

"Mom, Dad! Call the guards!" she yelled. She heard people yelling after her as she ran. She didn't care that people saw her in her nightgown; she just ran. She made it outside and to Oreck's cave. He was looking past her into the night and roaring loudly. She looked, too, and saw the undead man she'd seen in her head moments ago in her room, and suddenly, she saw ten more coming out from the shadows. She'd never seen this before.

"Oreck, remember the fire tornado we did? Let's do it again." She conjured up a huge windstorm, and Oreck breathed fire into it, and once more, they had a fire tornado. They raised another cyclone, and with Oreck, once again they had created another fire tornado. She moved her hands, pushing the tornadoes around the undead, swirling it around them and through them. They gave off a horrible shriek and burned into a crisp.

She could hear the horns blowing and her parents, along with Sandy and her mom, screaming at her. Her dad made the ground crumble under the undead, causing them to fall into this giant hole, and Sandy had lightning strike the undead as well, and then the soldiers started yelling "Fire!" She held her hand up to signal stop.

"Wait! I want to see if they are really dead!" she yelled out. They stopped. It went quiet, and after a few minutes, the undead started to rise again. Everlee knew what she had to do, but she'd never done it before. She always brought healing, but now she had to take away life, a life these creations shouldn't have been given. They were getting up and limping toward her now, getting closer, and Oreck was going forward. She touched him.

"No farther," she commanded. He stopped but continued to breathe fire at them and bare his fangs. She focused on the undead and concentrated so hard, willing their life forces to be stripped, leaving them a pile of truly dead bodies. She held her hand out, and after a few moments, they started to fall. Finally, they all hit the ground and a feeling washed over Everlee; she knew she had done it. She couldn't explain how. She walked toward the dead bodies.

"No, Everlee!" her parents and everyone screamed, but she didn't listen. She knew they were truly dead. She bent down and poked the front man with a stick. No sign of any movement; it was a dead corpse, and this time, they wouldn't come back. She knew she needed to burn the bodies to ash.

Oreck had followed her. "Burn them, Oreck. I'll help you. We'll do it together till they're nothing but ash." He started breathing fire on the bodies, and she sent fireballs at them, and after a time, they were nothing but ash.

"Princess," came Lieutenant Green's voice, "are you all right?"

"Yes, I'm fine, but we should be on the lookout for more tonight." He agreed.

Everlee's mom shot water over the burning mess and put it out before Everlee could, and then Evie walked over to her parents, Sandy, and Sandy's mom. They all came rushing toward her and hugged her and Oreck. "You could have been killed!" her mother exclaimed.

"But I wasn't. I can't explain it, Mom. I just knew it had to be me to stop them. Thank you all for your help though." They nodded.

"Of course, we couldn't let you face them alone. I'm sorry I couldn't do more, but I didn't want my water to put out your fire tornadoes."

"You're fine, Mom," Evie told her.

"Oh, Everlee, you were wonderful!" her father said, hugging her. "And so was Oreck. How did you know they were out here? He didn't start roaring till moments after you ran outside."

"Yeah, Evie, you bolted out of the room. Your eyes went all silver."

"I don't know, I had this feeling wash over me, and I knew Oreck needed me, and I saw through his eyes, I think. I saw the dead man before I ran out, and I know it had to be through Oreck's eyes 'cause he came out of the shadows a few seconds after I looked where Oreck was looking. They say dragons have excellent sight."

"How is that possible?" Sandy asked her.

"I don't know, but I'm glad I have that bond with him."

"But, Evie, I'm closely bonded to Cyrus too, but I've never shared his sight."

Evie shook her head. "I don't know."

"Well, let's get inside," her mother said, ushering them in.

"Not without Oreck, please. I know he's big, but please, he can sleep on my balcony, at least."

Her parents nodded. "The guards will stand watch tonight."

"I don't know how we're supposed to get sleep after this," Sandy muttered, walking inside.

Evie turned to Oreck. "Sleep on my balcony tonight, okay?" He roared and took off.

A little while later, the girls were in bed with guards outside the door and Cyrus and Oreck on the balcony. Sandy and Everlee lay facing each other. "Evie, I can't sleep."

"I know, I can't either."

"That was so terrifying, but you stayed so calm though."

"On the inside, I wasn't totally calm," Everlee said.

"Still, Evie, you were amazing. Are you gonna tell Dametri tomorrow?"

"Yes, definitely, and I want to talk to the headmaster."

"Don't worry," Sandy said, "I am sure he'll seek you out after hearing about this."

The girls eventually drifted off to sleep, although Everlee kept waking up in sweat and had a feeling that this was not the end, that more unpleasantries were coming this year.

Chapter 22

Finding Out Who Is Behind the Attacks

The girls woke up the next morning. Oreck and Cyrus were sleeping on the balcony. Thankfully, nothing else had happened. They went and washed up and came back and got dressed. Sandy's mom knocked on the door before entering. "Hey, girls," she said.

Evie liked Sandy's mom. She thought of her like an aunt, and Sandy wasn't a handmaiden anymore; she was now a guest for however long she liked and whenever she liked. They would always have a room for her, and her mom was now Everlee's mom's right hand; they were best friends too. Sandy's mom managed the staff. "How did you girls sleep?" Sandy's mother asked.

"It was really hard to fall asleep, but okay once I did," Sandy replied.

Her mom nodded. "And you, sweetie?"

Evie agreed with Sandy. She didn't want to scare them and tell them about the nightmares she had or about waking up in sweat and with a bad feeling. "Yeah, I just didn't sleep that well. I'm sure I'll be sleeping better in a few days." They nodded.

Together, they went down to breakfast. Oreck had woken up, as had Cyrus. They took off to go fly. After breakfast, they went to her father's study. Inside were her parents and the headmaster. "Hello, girls," Lional greeted them. Evie sat between her parents, and Sandy sat by her mom. "I heard about last night. I was just telling your parents there is only one person that could have done it—well, two, but Everlee would never." Everlee looked at him, and he continued, "I'm talking about Maureen, the elfin woman who had the gift before you my dear."

Sandy gasped. "So she's still alive then?"

"She must be to pull this off," said Lional, "but no one has seen her or Abraxas in fifty years. Anyway, I'll tell you more about her later, and I'll write to your parents about it later." The parents all nodded. "Now I've examined the ashes. Everlee, I'm very impressed. You've never had that type of training. How did you do it?"

She spoke up, "I don't know, sir. I just suddenly knew what to do. It came over me. I knew I had the means to end their lives and return them to death."

He nodded. "Interesting, and I heard you raised the alarm moments before Oreck was roaring."

She nodded. "I was in my room with Sandy, sir, and suddenly, I felt this bad feeling wash over me and knew Oreck needed me, and then I saw the undead man flash before my eyes, like I was looking through Oreck's eyes."

He nodded again, staring at her intently. "And you have never experienced this before?" he asked her.

"No, sir. The only thing we had was being able to know what Oreck's saying but not hearing him talking, but feeling his emotions, if you will, when I'm near him."

"Is that normal?" her father asked.

"Well, it's certainly new. No one else shares that strong of a connection, but for now, be glad she did. She and Oreck saved you all."

Her mother hugged her. "I'm just glad you're still here."

A little while later, they went outside and were outside Oreck's cave. Sandy and Everlee called for Oreck and Cyrus, who showed up after.

The headmaster turned the cave into a golden flaming portal like at the academy.

"Goodbye, Mom and Dad," Everlee said, hugging them. Then she hugged Sandy's mom, and Sandy hugged everyone too. "Oreck, you go first with Cyrus now." He roared, and the two of them went in and vanished. Sandy went next, followed by Everlee. They were back outside Oreck's cave now. When the headmaster popped out moments later, he turned it off, making it a normal cave again. Oreck roared happily and went in with Cyrus. They laughed.

"I think they want to get some good rest. I don't think they slept much," said Everlee.

They went back inside. "I'll see you girls tomorrow." Sandy looked confused. "Ms. Lewis, I am not naive to the fact that Ms. Everlee shares information with you. This way, you're just skipping a step and finding out together." They blushed. "But be careful who you share it with, understood?" They nodded. "Wonderful, now off you go. I'll send for you tomorrow."

They went to their room and lay down. "I'm gonna take a nap till dinner. I don't want lunch."

"Same here," said Sandy.

Later on, they awoke to a knock on their door. It was Kyle and Dametri. They hugged them.

"It's time for dinner, but we didn't see you, so we came to get you. Let's go eat." They followed the guys down to the dining hall. "So how was break?"

Before Sandy could speak, Everlee said, "Let's discuss that after dinner, please, in Oreck's cave for privacy. Dametri and Kyle looked worried but nodded.

After dinner, they were out in Oreck's cave. Rachel and Lacey were there as well; Sandy and Everlee had asked them to join them. "Now, you guys have to keep this quiet, for now at least." They nodded, looking worried. Everlee and Sandy told them about the other night. Dametri came over and hugged her tight. "But there's more."

Sandy looked. "What do you mean, Evie?"

"Sandy, please understand I didn't want to scare you this morning, okay?" She nodded. "Well, I kept having nightmares of what I saw last night." They nodded. "But that's not all, I kept waking up in a sweat and had this feeling wash over me that this is not the end." They looked worried.

"I don't know how you and Oreck can do what you do, but thank goodness you can," said Rachel, and everyone agreed.

"Well, there's more," said Everlee. "The headmaster thinks it's an elf named Maureen. She had the gift before me." Kyle and Lacey looked at each other.

"What is it?" Dametri said.

"Well," said Kyle, "Maureen disappeared fifty years ago, but elves live a very long time, so it's possible she's still alive. They don't talk about her much in the elfin village. They referred to her as the Mistress of Darkness."

Lacey piped up, "They say she used to be one of the kindest, purest souls, but that one day, something snapped and she started to change. They say she did horrible things before she disappeared."

Everyone sat in silence for a moment. "This is not good," said Sandy, and everyone nodded.

Rachel spoke up, "Why is she coming after you, Evie?"

Everlee then told them about the prophecy and that her parents thought she was the one. "If so, that's probably why."

"So she wants to eliminate the competition and what? Rule?" said Lacey.

"I wouldn't put it past her by the sound of things," Dametri said.

Evie nodded. "Well," Evie said, "she has another thing coming, 'cause I'm gonna keep fighting back. As future queen, I will not bow to her, and I will vanquish this darkness. I swear to you all." They all looked at her in awe.

"We're here for you, Everlee," Dametri said and kissed her. Everyone nodded and agreed.

Chapter 23

Happy Love Day

The next morning, Everlee and Sandy found themselves in the headmaster's office. "Hello, girls," Lional began, as he sat down behind his desk. Arden was perched on the back of his chair, looking at Cyrus on Sandy's shoulder. "Please tell me what you have learned from your friends yesterday." They looked at each other. "It's okay, girls, I expected it, just as long as they keep it quiet."

"They will," Evie said.

Sandy nodded. "Sir, how did you know?" Sandy asked.

"Well, intuition, and when I walked past the window and saw you guys all going in Oreck's cave, I had a feeling." He chuckled, and they blushed. "You're fine, ladies," he said. "So like I asked, what did you learn? Surely Kyle and Lacey have heard of Maureen."

Everlee nodded and spoke up, "Yes, sir. They agreed with you that she hasn't been around in fifty years and said the elves don't talk about her much other than referring to her as the Mistress of Darkness. I guess she used to be one of the kindest people, but something happened and she changed. They said she did horrible things."

Lional, who had been listening intently, spoke up, "Yes, that is all true, although clearly, some have seen her for this type of following to start and these events to happen." Sandy and Evie nodded. "I'm not sure what happened to her dragon, Abraxas. It's hard to hide a dragon, but

I can tell you this—she did do some terrible things. She was referred to as the Mistress of Darkness for a reason. She renounced her peaceful elfin ways and started a following. She thought those with gifts were superior and started killing and torturing people that would stand up to her. She wanted to rule, but she wouldn't have been a kind ruler. Your grandfather, Everlee, went to war with her, and the people rose up. She realized, I supposed, that the time wasn't right. Some say he injured her and she died, but clearly that's not the case. But, girls, I can't prove this, but I imagine she was there the other night—without her dragon, clearly. It's hard to hide one, and people would have noticed zombies marching through the kingdom."

"Then why didn't she fight me or raise more dead from the ground?" Everlee asked.

"I think she was testing you, and seeing how strong you are, you must have unnerved her, but I fear now that she knows how strong you are becoming, she will keep coming, my dear." Everlee sat there in shock. Sandy looked scared. "It's okay, girls, we won't back down, okay? For now, just go about your days, stay sharp, and come see me every so often, okay?" They nodded. "Very well, off you go." They said goodbye and took off.

As they walked off, Everlee found herself asking Sandy, "I wonder what made her snap and turn dark."

Sandy shook her head. "I don't want to think about her right now. By the sound of it, if she was there the other night, we're lucky she left."

Evie nodded. "I'm sorry, Sandy, I didn't mean to upset you."

"You're okay, Evie. I'm just trying to not think about it. I mean, what if she had won and killed you? I would have been heartbroken. I love you like a sister," said Sandy.

Evie stopped and hugged her. "Hey, it's okay. I'm right here, and I love you, too, very much. You're my soul sister."

"Okay." Sandy nodded, wiping away a single tear. "Can we just try to go back to normal and have fun, at least for a little while? She shouldn't ruin our lives when she's not here." Evie nodded, but she said that she was going to do research on her at the library. Sandy sighed. "If you must, but you won't forget to live and have fun too, right?"

Everlee nodded. "Yes, I'll have fun too." Sandy smiled, and then they headed back to class or at least what was left of weather class.

Time passed along without a hitch, and things were normal at the academy. The girls visited the headmaster twice. There was nothing new to report so far. It was now February, and it was Love Day. The girls were in Oreck's cave when they heard a knock on the outside. "Come in," Evie called.

In walked Kyle and Dametri. "There you girls are," said Kyle, giving Sandy a kiss, and Dametri kissed Everlee.

"Happy Love Day," the guys said.

"Happy Love Day," the girls echoed back.

"I have something for you," said Dametri, and out of his bag he pulled this lovely rose bouquet.

"It's beautiful," Evie said. "I love it!" And she kissed him. He grinned.

Kyle took the silence as his chance to tell Sandy he had something for her. "I asked Ms. Poppy, one of the cooks, to help me, and we made you cookies. They're sugar cookies and sweet, just like you." Sandy blushed as he took out a package from his bag, and she took one.

"It's so yummy!" she said after a bite. "Thank you."

"Sandy and I have something for you guys too."

"Ahh, you do?" Dametri grinned.

The girls laughed. "I'll see you later, Oreck. Enjoy your steak, okay? Happy Love Day." He grunted happily.

When they got outside, Sandy asked if she could go first. Everlee nodded. "Just keep it up after, okay?" Sandy nodded. "Our gifts are in two parts. Sandy and I wanted to do a show in the sky for you guys."

"Cool," they chorused.

They went over to the flower field. Sandy closed her eyes and, after a moment, opened them. They were purple. Suddenly, this huge rainbow appeared over the field. After a minute, her eyes went back to normal, but the rainbow was still there.

"Great job, Sandy." Evie smiled. "Okay, now for the finishing touch." Evie smiled. She stepped up and closed her eyes, willing and picturing what she wanted. She opened them, lifted her hands, and made a motion in front of her, and after a moment, she knew it had worked when she heard them gasp. Her eyes cleared. It worked! Up above the rainbow was lightning dancing; they were making the shape of hearts.

"Wow," said Dametri and Kyle together. The girls laughed. "So you like it?" said Sandy.

"I love it," said Kyle. "Thank you both," he said, kissing Sandy.

Dametri came over and placed his arms around Evie. "Thank you both," he said, and leaned down and kissed Everlee.

After a moment, Everlee looked at Sandy. "Ready for the last part?" She nodded, and the boys looked confused. "There's more?" said Kyle. They laughed and nodded.

Sandy turned back, raised her hands, and pushed toward the flowers. This caused all the petals to fall off; then simultaneously, Evie started making it snow. Sandy blew the flower petals up high, and they fell down with the snow.

"Neat," said Dametri.

"That's a sight," said Kyle.

"I agree. That is beautiful," said Lional. They turned, and sure enough, there was the headmaster. "Oh, I'm sorry for intruding. I just was walking outside when I saw the show. I hope that's okay." They all nodded.

"Oh, sir," said Everlee, "don't worry, I'll fix the flowers."

He laughed. "I'm sure you will. Beautiful show, girls." With that, he turned and left.

After a little while, they stopped the show but left the rainbow; it would go away in a few hours on its own. Everlee fixed the flower field; it was now full of beautiful flowers again.

They spent the rest of the day together. It was a Sunday, so they were all free to relax. Later that night, after dinner, they were back out to Oreck's cave with him. When the heard laughter and cawing, they went out and followed the sounds. It was Chad and Hannah; they were holding hands and laughing. Everlee spotted Midnight in the tree.

"Oh, I wonder where he's gone to. I'll find you, Midnight," said Chad. He kissed Hannah's hand and went toward the trees where Midnight stood out. Midnight cawed in a row, as if laughing, and Chad acted like he couldn't find him, clearly playing along. After a bit, he stopped and looked up and shouted "I found you!" to Midnight. Midnight cawed loudly and flew down. They went back to the cave after waving to Chad, Midnight, and Hannah.

"Those two are so cute," said Sandy.

"And Chad and Midnight are funny," said Kyle. Dametri and Everlee nodded in agreement.

Back inside, they stayed up chatting and telling jokes. Finally, the bell chimed. "Ugh," they groaned. They said good night to Oreck and Cyrus—he wanted to stay a bit longer with Oreck—and then they went back to their rooms and kissed their boyfriends good night. Kyle and Dametri walked off, and Everlee closed the door.

"That was perfect," Sandy cooed, looking all smitten.

Everlee laughed. "Yes, it was," she agreed.

They changed into their pajamas, and when Cyrus flew in and landed on Sandy's bed, Sandy went over and stroked his feathers. Everlee heard Oreck and pulled the curtains back. "Good night, Oreck. I love you." She hugged him as best she could, and he roared happily and took off. The girls went to bed shortly after that.

Chapter 24

Time Gone By and a Surprise

It was now April 14. Over the last two months, things had been normal. Classes passed by like usual. The wolves in the prison still wouldn't talk even though her father and Lieutenant Green told Borris they knew Maureen was behind things and asked why they followed her, but they refused to speak, and Jack wasn't talking much. He did ask about his familiar and was happy he was safe, but her father said you could see the sadness in his eyes. Jack asked about his parents, and her father told him that they were doing all right but that they missed him and wished he talked. Her father said, after that, all Jack would say was "I'm sorry, I wish I could, and I never wanted this." Her father felt maybe Jack would start talking soon.

As far as her friends, Valerie was still single. She said her date was nice but that she was happy doing her own thing. Grace, too, was happy being single. Hannah and Chad were so cute together. Sandy and Kyle were still very much in love, and Everlee could tell they will marry after they graduated in a little over three years. Lacey was now dating Oliver as of last week; he seemed nice so far. Rachel and Rowland had a blast back at the dance in December and were now a couple as well. As far as Aiden and Robert, those two were fine staying single right now. As for her and Dametri, things were wonderful. He was the one; she could feel it.

Later that day, she found herself in the library. She was determined to find out more about Maureen. There had to be some more information in a book there, and she was going to find it. A while later, she found a book that looked promising, and after she checked it out and was leaving, she heard Midnight cawing, followed by the librarian, Ms. Chow, exclaiming "This is a library!" before storming off in Midnight's direction. Evie laughed as she left. Ms. Chow wasn't thrilled with Midnight, but Midnight was just so full of life and had to share it very loudly in the library. He seemed to like Ms. Chow because whenever she would come over to shush him, he cawed happily at her, which didn't help things.

On her way back to her room, Everlee ran into Dametri. "Hey," she said. He hugged and kissed her. He looked at the book in her arms. "Did you find more information on Maureen?" he asked her.

"I hope so," Everlee replied. "I'll let you know if I do after I read it." He nodded. "So what were you up to?" she asked him. "I'd tell you about my evening, but I'm pretty sure you can guess I was at the library."

He chuckled. "I was just writing my dad a letter. He wrote to me, and so far, my older brother is still not acting himself, so if he isn't better by summer break, he's out of the running for beta."

Evie shook her head. "I'm so sorry," she said.

"It's not your fault. Let's go outside for a bit. We still have about thirty minutes. We can visit Oreck."

"Okay." She nodded. Sasha found them as soon as they made it outside. She ran up to Dametri and sat on his shoulder, chattering away all happy-like. He laughed. "Hey, girl," he said, petting her head. They walked over to Oreck's cave, and just before they went inside, Gertie showed up with her group of girls.

"Hey, Gertie," he said.

"Hey," she replied with a smile. "What are you up to?"

"Not much," Evie spoke up, demanding her presence be known, "just spending time as a couple."

"How quaint," Gertie said. "Well, see you, Dametri." She grinned and waved before taking off.

Everlee and Dametri turned and went inside. Oreck was thrilled to see them. He was now almost double his size before break. It wouldn't be long before he was fully grown. He and Dametri had gotten to be good friends.

"So out of curiosity, what are Gertie's talents?" Evie asked.

"She has earth and fire," said Dametri. "Same as me, except I have one extra talent, water." Evie nodded to show she understood.

Later on, they bid Oreck good night, and Dametri walked Everlee to her room. She kissed him good night. She went inside, closed the door behind her, and got into her pajamas. She walked across the hall to use the bathroom and came back, but just before she opened her door, Sandy showed up.

"Hey, Evie," said Sandy.

"Hey." Evie smiled. They went inside.

"So how was your day?" Sandy asked as she changed into her pajamas.

"It was good," said Evie. "I found a book in the library that looks promising, so I'm looking forward to reading it."

Sandy shuddered. "I hope we don't see her or any of her dark plans anytime soon."

"I know," said Evie, "but I have to know my enemy."

Sandy nodded. "I get it," she said. "I just don't like thinking about her." Evie hugged her. Cyrus suddenly flew in and landed on Sandy's pillow, causing her to chuckle. "Well, someone's ready for bed, I see," Sandy said to Cyrus. He hooted back.

Everlee walked over to the window and pulled the curtain back, and just before she was about to call for Oreck, he appeared. "Hey, big guy," she said, hugging him as best she could. "I love you." He grunted happily. "All right, you head off to bed, okay?" He roared a happy sound and took off. She knew he understood her. She was blessed to have him, and she knew he felt blessed to have her too.

Everlee turned off all but one light on the desk between them and lit a fire in the fireplace. She got into bed and lay down. "What about your book, aren't you gonna read?" asked Sandy.

"Tomorrow," said Everlee, "I just feel so tired suddenly."

Sandy nodded. "Yeah, me too, Evie." And shortly after, they drifted off to sleep.

A while later, Everlee awoke. It was still dark out. She looked over at Sandy; she was still fast asleep. Everlee had class in a few hours, and Evie knew she should go back to bed, but she had another strange feeling come over her. She got up and went to the window. She had just heard Oreck roar, and the other familiars were going off too. She pulled back the curtain and looked outside, but regretted it when she spotted a pair of eyes staring back at her in the woods. It was an elfin woman, but something was radiating off her that screamed darkness. Evie screamed. The elfin woman smiled and walked off. Sandy woke up, and Oreck heard her yells and was suddenly at her window too, roaring.

Chapter 25

Telling the Academy

Sandy awoke to Everlee's scream. "What's the matter?" she yelled. Cyrus was going nuts too.

"I think I just saw Maureen!" said Evie. Sandy went ghost white. Suddenly, Everlee snapped back to reality. "Oh my gosh! I have to go after her," she said and started toward the door.

Sandy jumped out of bed, ran, and stood in front of the door. "No, Evie!" she yelled, crying. "No, please, you're not running off on your own and into what could be a trap! You're strong, but so is she. Please don't!" Sandy wept and hugged her.

Evie felt bad. "I'm sorry, Sandy, I just hate letting her walk away."

"I know," Sandy sniffled. "But I can't lose you. You'll face her head-on someday, I think, but not tonight, not like this." Evie nodded. She agreed in her head with Sandy's words; she would face Maureen one day, and she was gonna win.

Oreck and Cyrus were still all worked up when they heard a knock. Sandy opened the door; it was the headmaster. "Girls, please put on your robes. All students are going to the dining hall."

"But, sir, she's out there. I saw her," said Everlee. "I saw Maureen. At least, I'm pretty sure it was her. It was an elfin woman, and I felt darkness coming off her."

He looked concerned. "That was who was out there?" Lional asked her.

Evie nodded. "Yes, sir, I'm pretty sure." She opened the book and scrolled through it fast. "Yes, she's in here!" she screamed. She turned the book to the headmaster. "That's her, that's Maureen. I saw her outside," she said, showing the picture of Maureen.

"Okay, that's it," he said, "to the dining hall, quickly."

The girls put on their robes. Evie bid Oreck goodbye for now, and Cyrus flew onto Sandy's shoulder. They locked the door behind them and followed the headmaster.

The halls were full of students rubbing their eyes and looking confused, and some even looked scared. Rachel and Lacey spotted Evie and Sandy by Lional and ran over. "Walk and talk, please, ladies," said Lional, ushering them forward along with the teachers.

"What's going on?" Rachel said. Everlee saw, but Evie shook her head no.

Sandy stopped. "I'll tell you later," she whispered. "Too many people around, it would cause a panic."

Lacey paled. "It's that bad?" Everlee nodded.

They all made it to the dining hall and sat down. Minutes later, Kyle, Rowland, and Dametri joined them and Valerie. After everyone was inside, the headmaster and the teachers went up front. The two warrior sergeants for day and night guard stood by the hall doors. Everyone was whispering and looking around. Lional stood up in his seat, magically magnified his voice, and began speaking.

"Now I know it's very late, and I am sure you're all wondering what's going on and why the familiars were going off." Everyone nodded. "I'll tell you," he began. "We had someone standing in the woods staring up at a student's room. This person is very bad and dangerous. All the familiars did an excellent job alerting us. Please stay focused on me and be as quiet as you can, please, till I am finished. I want you all to know what's going on so that you can protect yourselves and stay out of danger."

He began talking about last October and told them that Jack had been working for someone. They found out who, and he told about the undead attack at Everlee's home during winter break, which caused lots of stares in her direction. Lional cleared his throat. "Look at me, please. Now tonight, we believe that the main culprit behind everything was in the woods. She was staring at Everlee's room, and her name is Maureen, the Mistress of Darkness as others know her." There were gasps and a few screams. "Now some of you know about her, and some don't. She, too, has the gift of regeneration and a dragon named Abraxas. She, prior to these events, has not been seen for fifty years, and now hear this, she is not to be approached. If you see her, get away." They nodded. "She is evil and dark. She will lie to you and deceive you. She will only bring misery. Everlee, my dear, please stand up and tell us what you saw of her so we know what to look for."

Everlee stood up, and Dametri held her hand for comfort. She was a bit shaken and wasn't expecting the headmaster to tell everyone, but he was right; they needed to know. "Well, she was not that close, but from the glow of the academy, I saw that she had light-black skin and long silver hair to the middle of her chest. She had green eyes, I think—"

Kyle interrupted, "Yes, she does. They say they're as green as emeralds . . . uh, sorry, Everlee." He blushed and quieted down.

"It's okay," she said. "And she was just radiating darkness." Everlee sat back down.

"What about her dragon?" a second-year girl shouted.

"I didn't see a dragon," Everlee said.

The headmaster carried on, "Thank you, Everlee. Now, students, we are unsure if her dragon is alive or not, but even if he isn't, she is very dangerous. Let's not forget that Everlee is our future queen." They nodded. "Her dragon, Oreck, is growing every day, and he is strong, and Everlee is gifted with all the talents, which is something no one else has, not even Maureen. What I read was she only has four talents, one of which is regeneration.

"There was a prophecy that one would be born in the winter with the potential to be the greatest around. I believe strongly, without any doubt, that it refers to Everlee, and that is a comfort. Others like Maureen are likely targeting her because they know, as she grows, she'll get stronger and will one day be able to defeat them. Maureen is clearly seeing Everlee as a threat, which should comfort you to have such a strong and capable future queen. I encourage you all to stand by her and stay true and loyal. Even if some of you don't care for her, you should still stand true." The students nodded. "Now is when we need to stand together. Things could heat up in the next few days or as long as years before we see a huge battle, and if we stay united, we are strong. Now stay calm, please, the night sergeant and I are going to go look around the grounds to make sure everything is all clear."

There was a knock on the hall door, and the students screamed. "Silence!" Lional projected. "It's only the palace guard. I heard the alarms go off and sent a fast note asking for some backup." They calmed, and most seemed happy to hear about having backup. The headmaster walked through the hall, stopped by Evie real quick, and whispered in her ear, "I'm sorry I couldn't warn you beforehand, but I thought they should know." She nodded. He squeezed her shoulder and walked forward and out the hall with the night sergeant. The doors closed, leaving them with the teachers and the day sergeant, Ms. Hyde.

Valerie looked at her. Hannah and Grace came over, and they asked why she never told them. "I'm sorry. I wanted to, but I didn't want to scare anyone." They nodded.

"No more secrets," Grace pleaded, and Evie nodded. They seemed pleased.

After what felt like forever, the headmaster returned and, magnifying his voice, announced there was no sign of Maureen. "You may all go back to bed. Classes are cancelled for today, and the extra guards will be standing guard around the outside of the academy and staying with us till further notice. Now off to bed you go."

Everyone stood up and walked off. Dametri and Everlee said goodbye and kissed real quick before parting. Everlee walked to her room with Sandy. They got to their room and got in bed.

Oreck was not outside. *He must be in his cave again,* Everlee thought. The girls lay there talking and trying to fall asleep. Eventually, they did and awoke to knocking. Everlee answered it. Outside the door was Rachel. "Let's get breakfast," she said.

"Okay, come in. Sandy and I have to change real quick." The girls got dressed, and together they left for breakfast, locking up behind them.

Chapter 26

Taking a Ride

After breakfast, Everlee went back to her room. There was a lot of staring, and she wanted to finally read that book she found yesterday. She got to her room and closed her door, but before she sat down with the book, she went to her window and called out for Oreck. He came right away. "Hey, boy," she said, stroking his head. "Thanks for last night." He grunted. "We have to stay sharp, okay?" He leaned into her hand as if agreeing. "Well, I'm gonna read for a bit, but I'll be out later today, okay?" He roared his approval and took off. She smiled, turned and grabbed the book, and sat on her bed.

She read and read until it was lunchtime. Before she took off for lunch, she sat and thought about what she had read. She was right—this book did talk about Maureen. It told Everlee what Maureen's four talents were—water, wind, fire, and regeneration. It told how, when Maureen was in school, she was a model student, and then about after she graduated, she was known for her kindness. It stated that, for reasons unknown, she started to change and did all these horrific acts, and that Everlee's grandfather went to war with her, and that she and Abraxas disappeared. No one knows if she and Abraxas are still alive.

Well, Everlee thought, *we know she's still alive, that's for sure, and I guess we'll find out about Abraxas one day.* She wondered if she would ever find out what caused the change in Maureen, who was known for her kindness. What happened? Everlee wasn't giving up; she'd find out one day.

Everlee went, closed her door and locked it behind her, and went to lunch. After lunch, she and Dametri went for a walk outside. They went to Oreck's cave, only this time, she called for Oreck to walk with her and Dametri. They strolled over to the side of the academy, by her window. The guards were still around. She told them she wanted to see where Maureen had stood. They didn't want to, for safety, but let her, with two guards going with them.

She went to where she had seen Maureen standing; there was nothing there. "Oh well," she sighed. Everlee and the others left. The guards went back to their posts, and Everlee and Dametri enjoyed the rest of their day with Oreck and Sasha.

Everything went back to normal slowly. It was now the end of May. They had a week of school left before summer break.

"The year went by fast," said Sandy at lunch.

"Yeah, it did," agreed Everlee.

They had a written test in each class coming up on Wednesday, and then on Friday, they would go home. They spent time together with their boyfriends and friends and, of course, studying. As usual, Midnight was still driving the librarian nuts, which was always good for a chuckle.

It was now Wednesday, and Everlee and Sandy were finished with their exams. They passed them all.

"Thank goodness," Sandy gasped. Evie agreed.

The next day, Thursday, the girls finished packing. They had been working on it a little bit here and there for a few days. They went down to lunch and enjoyed a delicious meal of fried chicken and mashed potatoes with corn. Then Everlee, Dametri, and her friends all went outside. They went to the field, and all hung out for their last afternoon.

Tomorrow after breakfast, they would all be leaving, and like last time, Everlee and Sandy would go first through Oreck's cave. Grace and Hannah were braiding each other's hair and laughing over some joke. Rachel and Rowland were lying by each other. Lacey was off walking on a trail with her boyfriend, and Sandy and Kyle were playing with their familiars. Meanwhile, the rest of the familiars were playing together or enjoying the weather.

Everlee was leaning against Dametri's chest and watching Oreck fly. She was amazed at his size. She had watched him grow from an egg. He was still less than a year old, but as it may, he was finally fully grown and had become huge. She didn't know how to describe his size.

Suddenly, Headmaster Lional showed up. "Good day, my students," he greeted them. They smiled at him. "Hello," they chorused. Arden was, as usual, on his shoulder. Lional looked up at Oreck. "My, has he grown."

"Yes," said Everlee. "I want to try to ride him. If he lets me, how far can I fly?"

Lional smiled. "Just follow Arden, and when I call Arden down, you come down too, you promise?" She nodded happily. "Very well then." He smiled. "Let's call Oreck down and see what happens, shall we?" She nodded and stood up.

"Oreck!" she yelled up to him. He turned at his name and came down to the ground. She walked up to him and stroked his head and neck once he lowered it for her. Lional walked over too. "Hey, big guy, I was wondering if I could ride you?" He put his head against hers as if saying yes and gave a happy roar. She smiled. "Thank you," she told him. She looked to Lional and nodded.

He grinned. "Very well then, up you get." Luckily, Evie was wearing a pair of pants and a shirt. She had Oreck lower himself down all the way and carefully climbed on his back. He had small spikes on his back that she held on to.

"Now follow Arden, okay?" she said. "He's the hawk." Oreck grunted. "We're ready," Everlee said.

Everyone was watching. Her friends had stopped and came to watch. Even Lacey was there now with her boyfriend, as they were done with the trail. Lional turned his head to Arden. "Lead them around the academy, but not too far away, and come back when I call." Arden screeched and took off.

Suddenly, Oreck flew up in the air. "Whoa!" Evie yelled. Her stomach flipped. Oreck followed Arden around over some of the woods and the trails. She heard people cheering and happily yelling down below. "This is wonderful!" Everlee exclaimed to Oreck. He roared happily. He seemed just as thrilled to have her in the air with him.

After a while, Arden must have heard Lional because he descended, and so did they. Arden landed on Lional's shoulder. "Good job, Arden," Lional said to him, and Everlee and Oreck landed too. "You two were fabulous! How was it?" he said, coming over to give her a hand down.

She took his hand. "It was amazing!" Everlee exclaimed. She hugged Oreck. "Oh, thank you so much!" she said. "Okay, sweet boy, you can go play now." He roared happily and took off into the sky.

Dametri and her friends all surrounded her and hugged her, and they chatted about it. Headmaster Lional took off.

The next day, after breakfast, Sandy and Everlee walked down to Oreck's cave. Dametri and Kyle pulled them aside really fast. Kyle kissed Sandy, and Dametri kissed Everlee. "I love you, stay in touch," he told her.

"I love you too," she told him, "and I will, I promise." He smiled and took off. She waved goodbye.

Sandy bid Kyle goodbye too, and minutes later, they were at Oreck's cave. It was already full of gold flames. Everlee called Oreck down from the sky. Their luggage wasn't there. Headmaster Lional must have guessed because he grinned and said, "Your luggage was just sent off a few minutes ago. Ms. Love and my son brought them down for you."

"Please thank them," Sandy said.

Lional nodded. "I'll see you girls next school year, and sooner, if problems arise—but let's hope they don't." The girls nodded.

"You first, Oreck," Everlee said. He roared, went in, and disappeared. Sandy and Cyrus went next, then Everlee walked forward.

"Goodbye, sir," she said to the headmaster.

He smiled. "Goodbye, my dear, until the fall."

She smiled, walked into the flames, and disappeared. She couldn't wait. The academy was an amazing place, and it had become a second home to her.

CPSIA information can be obtained
at www.ICGtesting.com
Printed in the USA
BVHW032100270319
543866BV00003B/7/P